CAUGHT!

Willie screamed.

"Mr. Gordon! Look!"

Flash wheeled. Willie was pointing to a pile of boulders beside the pathway, over which three figures were climbing. The figures wore hoods and brilliant electric-blue robes, tied with a golden chain at the waist. Their faces were invisible inside the dark hoods, wreathed as they were in some kind of blue gauze, but Flash could discern gleaming eyes and bright teeth behind the drawn-back lips.

"An ambush," snapped Flash. *"And we've got no weapons."*

OTHER FLASH GORDON ADVENTURES from Avon Books

FLASH GORDON

The Witch Queen of Mongo

Alex Raymond's original story
Adapted by Carson Bingham

Co-published by Avon Books
and King Features Syndicate

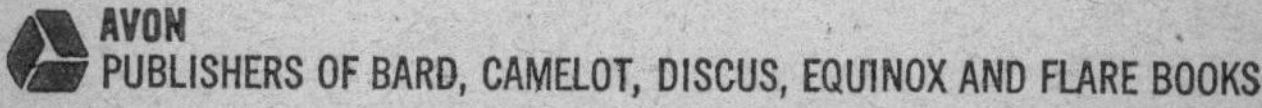

THE WITCH QUEEN OF MONGO
is an original publication of Avon Books.
This work has never before appeared in book form.

AVON BOOKS
A division of
The Hearst Corporation
959 Eighth Avenue
New York, New York 10019

Co-published by Avon Books and King Features Syndicate, Inc.

ISBN: 0-380-00180-2 

First Avon Printing, December, 1974.

AVON TRADEMARK REG. U.S. PAT. OFF. AND
FOREIGN COUNTRIES, REGISTERED TRADEMARK—
MARCA REGISTRADA, HECHO EN CHICAGO, U.S.A.

Printed in the U.S.A.

Chapter 1

Heat lightning flashed beyond Black Hat Mountain, silhouetting the low-lying desert-ranch laboratory of Dr. Hans Zarkov in the distance. From twenty miles away in the flat empty desert, Flash Gordon saw the outlines of the buildings and turned to Dale Arden beside him in the seat of the X-905 WM Sport Car.

"We're almost there, Dale," he said with a smile. "I hope this puts an end to your worries about our safety."

Flash was a strapping young man with curly blond hair, blue eyes, and an engaging smile. He was dressed in loose-fitting sports clothes with an open collar and trim slacks.

"Go on," Dale said ruefully. "Tell me I'm just a silly girl. But I've been feeling very odd about this trip."

She was a slender, dark-haired girl in her early twenties, slightly tall for a woman, but pleasantly feminine in an outdoorsy way. Dressed in a short skirt and blouse, she was a perfect specimen of the Earth female.

"Come on," said Flash, trying to tease his companion out of her strange mood. "We'll be there in a few minutes. Doc Zarkov will tell us why he invited us out on such short notice, and we can all sit back and have a good laugh at your fears."

"I hope so," said Dale between pinched lips. She glanced again out into the darkness of the desert, which stretched away into vast emptiness all around them. In the distance to the rear of them, she could see the vague glow of Megalopolis West, which they had left over two hours before.

Flash sighed. "All right. Out with it. What do you think is bothering you?"

"I think someone is watching us, Flash," said Dale. "I can't help it."

Flash waved his arm vaguely toward the vast space about them. "Now who could be doing that? You can see for miles."

"I know," Dale said worriedly. "But I can't get it out of my mind."

The X-905 WM zoomed along the flat road that cut across the desert as straight as an arrow.

"If only Doc Zarkov wasn't such a boor about his darned old lab," she complained, snorting. "We could fly in with one of the aircars. But no—he's got to have all that security nonsense—radar traps, anti-magnetic nets, the works."

"You know Doc," Flash said gently.

"He could have turned off all the scanners until we got down safely," she said, grumbling. "But no, he makes us crawl to him in an ordinary terrestrial car!"

"I haven't seen Doc for six months, Dale. I'll be glad to see him. I don't know what's gotten into you."

Dale shrugged. "I don't either." She looked about her again suspiciously. "There's something out there, Flash."

It was extremely dark in the desert where Flash was driving between Megalopolis West and Zarkov's famous ZZZ Rancho in the middle of the Mojave Desert, USA, Earth. It was eleven-thirty at night. He had gotten the vidphone call from Zarkov at about nine and had then picked up Dale at the World Council Building, where they both now worked, and had driven across the valley and into the mountains in his X-905 Sport Car, the newest World Motors model for terrestrial driving.

"Did he give you any hint about what he wants to show us?" Dale asked.

"No."

Dale sat there rigidly, with her hands clasped in her lap. "I hope it's not one of those bothersome practical jokes of his."

Flash did not have time to respond. The transformation occurred so suddenly that he did not even see the change in the landscape or in the lighting. That is, there was no end to the night and the desert and no beginning to the brightly lighted, strange, indescribable terrain through which they were driving.

"Flash!" Dale gasped, her eyes wide.

Flash turned to her with a frown. "What happened?"

"I—I don't know!"

Instinctively Flash slowed down the X-905 and stared out at the strange terrain. It did not resemble earth at all, or wilderness, or even a moonscape of mineral formations. It was indeed a most strange and unbelievable sight. It seemed to Flash, in his dazed mind, that they were driving through a giant mound of ice cream topped with chocolate sauce and a bright red maraschino cherry.

The car rolled to a stop.

Flash flipped the OFF switch.

He stared out the side of the car.

"I'd swear I was having an hallucination," he said, half to himself.

"Me, too," said Dale. "It—it looks like—an—"

They both said it together: "An ice-cream sundae!"

Dale sat up straight. "It's one of Zarkov's little tricks, you can bet on that. Mass hypnotism, perhaps."

Flash nodded. "I think you may be right."

He glanced out once again, and the scene had not appreciably changed. The ice-cream terrain rose from the pavement upon which the car rested, sloping up into a rounded mound on each side of them. A huge layer of what seemed to be chocolate sauce extended to the top of the hills on both left and right.

Flash opened the car door. "I'm going to find out what this is all about," he snapped.

Dale said nothing. She was staring out her window at the bizarre landscape.

There was a brightness in the air, but when Flash looked up there was no sun. The atmosphere seemed to be indirectly lighted all around, as if they were in some special world that needed no sun or moon.

"What's this?" Flash muttered and looked down at his feet. He had stepped out of the car onto the pavement, which he had supposed to be the same macadam upon which they had been driving. But it had changed. Indeed it resembled a kind of licorice.

He bent down and touched it with his fingers. The material was slick and slightly pliant, and when he took away his fingers and held them to his nose he knew he had been right—he could smell the unmistakable odor of licorice.

He touched his tongue to his finger. "It's licorice, Dale!"

"What are you saying?"

"The pavement—it's licorice!"

"Licorice?" she repeated, suddenly realizing that she had not been imagining what he said.

"Licorice."

She opened the door unbelievingly and stepped out, frowning in bewilderment. She, too, bent down to touch the licorice pavement.

"It's mad!" she whispered.

Flash had turned to study the strange landscape formation stretching away from the licorice pavement. He walked over to it and touched it.

Then he turned around and stared at Dale. "You won't believe me, but it's vanilla ice cream, Dale."

Dale's face turned white. "I knew you were going to say that."

Now Flash's eyes discerned a break in the creamy surface of the terrain and he began walking along the pavement toward it.

Dale caught up with him. "What's that shape?"

"I'm going to find out," said Flash.

As they approached the formation, they could see that it resembled a kind of milky crystal. The shape of the material hinted at mineral formation, but as they got closer to it they saw that it was not rock at all, but something approximating rock.

They stood by the waist-high crag for a long moment before Flash had the nerve to put out his hand to touch it.

"Dale," he whispered, "you know what this is?"

She shook her head, almost fearfully.

"Have you ever eaten rock candy?"

Dale blinked. "Yes. When I was a kid we used to have it once in a while. It's just boiled sugar, isn't it? Boiled sugar dried out on strings until it crystallizes?"

"That's right," said Flash. He touched the rocklike excrescence and then put his finger to his lips once again. "Rock candy, Dale."

She moved past him and touched the rocklike formation too, tasting it.

They both stared at one another.

Then Flash said, "That's it! That's it!"

"What?"

"We're in it now. The Big Rock Candy Mountain!"

Dale stared at him as if he were bereft of his senses. "The Big Rock Candy Mountain? Are you crazy?"

"Maybe I am," said Flash, half-laughing. "But that's

where we are. There was an old song: 'The Big Rock Candy Mountain.' It's what every child imagines when he's a kid. Going to a place where there are lollypops for trees, where there are streams of soda, lakes of chocolate sauce, and ice-cream houses."

"But it's only in someone's imagination, Flash," Dale said in a whisper.

Flash nodded. He turned and looked up along the curved slope of the ice-cream hill.

"But how did we get here?" he asked.

"And how do we get out?" Dale asked, shuddering to herself. "Why, it's like being inside someone's diseased mind!"

Flash stared at her. "Diseased? A man's mind might be diseased, thinking of this. But not a child's mind, Dale. If it were a child's mind, it could be a very healthy one."

Dale blinked. "Doc Zarkov? Some scheme of his? Putting us into someone's imagination?"

"I don't know," Flash said, shaking his head. "It's beyond me." He took Dale's hand. "Come on, let's go back to the car."

"But what are we going to do?"

"Just drive along the road and see where it leads," he said.

Dale thought a moment. "I guess that's all we can do."

They went back to the car. For a moment, Flash stood by it and then walked over to the side of the road.

"What are you going to do?" Dale asked.

"I'm going to sample this stuff and see if it's real, too, or only an hallucination."

Dale came over by him. "I want to try it, too."

Flash leaned down and scooped up a bit of the ice-cream substance in his hand and began licking it slowly.

"Vanilla," he said. "And a very good flavor of it, too."

Dale ate some of the ice cream. "I've never really tasted such a fine flavor."

Flash sighed. "Come on. Let's get back in the car and see what's next in this programmed little game."

Dale turned to him. "You think—?"

"It's Doc Zarkov, all right! I only wish I knew what he's trying to prove."

They climbed into the car and Flash started it up. They moved down the licorice highway for a half mile, and now they could see brightly colored lollypops on the side of the road, forming a kind of candy forest. They crossed a bridge then, made of hard-candy cane rails and chocolate logs. Under the bridge a stream of what was obviously sparkling soda pop flowed along merrily over candied boulders. A great excrescence of gumdrop rocks was strewn over a hillside that looked like pulled taffy.

Then suddenly there was laughter—booming, familiar laughter.

"Doc Zarkov, you fiend!" cried Flash, half in jest. "What is this latest trick of yours?"

Dale screamed.

Flash could feel the wheel in his hand turn to licorice whips. And now he could see that the car itself had turned into a different kind of material—hard, white, Easter-egg chocolate with whipped-cream upholstering.

Yet they continued riding merrily along.

"I don't believe it!" yelled Flash.

And next to him he could hear Dale Arden weeping in sudden fear.

"We've gone mad, Flash. Mad!"

The sky above them suddenly began melting and the car itself was disintegrating at the speed it was traveling. The ice-cream hills rolled down toward them, and they were both sinking down and down into a morass of sugar and cream and chocolate.

And then, quite suddenly, they were seated quietly in a familiar room.

"Well," said Doc Zarkov, grinning at them in that maudlin and exasperating way he had, "how did you like that exhibition?"

And he threw back his head and laughed uproariously.

Chapter 2

Dr. Hans Zarkov, a large burly man with a big black beard and intelligent dark eyes, folded his arms across his chest and smiled broadly.

"Don't look so baffled, my friends," he told Flash and Dale.

Flash rose from the chair in which he had just discovered himself, and advanced toward Zarkov. "Doc, is this another of your fool tricks? And if it is—how does it work?"

Zarkov lifted his head and boomed with laughter. "Pretty mystifying, isn't it?"

The dark-haired girl shifted in her chair and snapped, "Doc, you're a child at heart. Do you know that? You'll never grow up."

Zarkov's eyes widened innocently. "What's the matter, Dale? You seem put out." He laughed loudly again, rubbing his fingers across his black beard.

"What was it?" Flash asked, standing close to Zarkov, almost threateningly. "Tele-hypnosis?"

Zarkov waved Flash back, his eyes betraying a fear that Flash would bodily attack him in his massive annoyance. "Sit down, Flash. Calm yourself."

Flash stared and then retreated.

Zarkov moved about the spacious quarters of his desert laboratory's living room, peering once out into the darkened night, and then wheeling to face Flash and Dale, muscular arms folded over his barrel chest. He was wearing a light-colored sport shirt and tapered slacks that fitted into leather desert boots.

"Well, now," he drawled. "I could have put you two under hypnosis once you arrived her, told you to forget the last ten minutes of your drive across the desert, and made you imagine your drive through the strange land of ice cream and candy, you know."

"Darn you, Doc," Flash growled, half-rising from his chair. "If you're going to play games—"

"No games," Zarkov retorted hastily. "I say, I *could* have done the trick by using posthypnotic suggestion. Right?"

"Right," Dale said calmly. "But you didn't."

"That's right, I didn't." Zarkov moved across the room and stared down at his two friends. "Ever hear of psychokinesis?"

"Sure," said Flash. "It's the power of the mind to move objects about in space."

"Right. It's a kind of active extrasensory perception. Very little is actually understood about it. But it is scientifically known to exist."

Flash frowned. "But I don't see how—"

"Let me finish," Zarkov said, smiling. "Closely allied to extrasensory perception is clairvoyance, the power of seeing something which is distant from one and out of his sight."

"That's basic science," Flash said, snorting.

"Don't be impatient, my friend," said Zarkov. "Clairvoyance is the power to receive a picture of something not in one's sight. We don't know enough about ESP to understand it clearly, as I said, and we don't actually know how it works."

Dale nodded.

"And we don't really know enough about ESP to be sure a person can't send a message to someone else by telepathy, now, do we?"

"Okay, Doc," Flash said. "Are you telling me you sent us a message to drive through the Big Rock Candy Mountain?"

Zarkov stroked his beard thoughtfully. "Not exactly," he said. "But by adding up the facts of ESP, we do conclude that such a thing might be possible. Right?"

"Oh, sure," snapped Flash. "I'll concede it might be possible."

Zarkov chuckled gleefully.

Dale sat up straight in her chair, her dark eyes wide. "But you have done it to us!"

"I haven't," Zarkov said softly. "But somebody else has."

"Who?" Flash frowned.

Zarkov moved over to Flash and stood above him. "First, I want you to admit that you could have been involved in a kind of telepathic delusion."

Flash frowned. "Oh, all right. I'll concede that."

"And then I want you to promise me not to laugh at my—my subject."

"Who is it?" Dale asked.

Zarkov turned and looked at the far door, which Flash knew led to one of the three bedrooms in the house. "Willie!" he called.

A short silence.

The door opened slowly. Flash and Dale watched it with intense concentration.

Through the opening stepped a gangling, thin, youthful figure of a teenage youngster, about fifteen, who stood there for a moment in painful embarrassment. His face turned rapidly red and he looked at the floor shyly.

He seemed all bone and elbows, with long arms, long legs, and a long thin neck. His head was almost too heavy for his body and the ears again almost too large for the head. He had curly red hair that stood out from his skull and freckles on his rather blank-looking face. His eyes were green and vacant, almost as if his thoughts were never very clearly in focus.

He wore a tee shirt and bright-colored slacks, with a belt that was too big for his waist and pulled tight through extra loops in the pants.

"Willie," Zarkov said. "I'd like you to meet some good friends of mine."

Flash was surprised at the difference in Zarkov's usual effusive, booming manner. He now seemed quite cool and polite.

The youth lifted his head and looked at Zarkov, then at Flash, and then at Dale. When he saw Dale, he colored again immediately, and looked away quickly.

"Flash Gordon," said Zarkov, "and Dale Arden."

Willie lifted his head and started walking across the room toward them. "How do you do?" he said awkwardly. His voice had not yet changed fully, and the words came out squeakily.

Flash stood and held out his hand. "Hi, Willie."

"Mr. Gordon," said Willie.

The hand that Flash gripped was strong and painfully fleshless.

Willie then turned to Dale. He made an almost courtly little bow. "Miss Arden," he said.

Dale laughed and held out her hand. "Hello, Willie."

Willie took the hand and blushed once again.

"His full name is William Edgar Casey," Zarkov announced. "But he's known as Willie. Worriless Willie."

Willie flushed and stood back from the group.

"Worriless?" Flash asked.

"He doesn't have any worries," said Zarkov with a kindly chuckle. "He's a dreamer," he continued with a glance at Willie. Willie looked at the floor. "That's why they sent him to me, actually. Figured I could make something out of him."

"You're an astrophysicist, a nuclear engineer, and a space scientist, Doc," Dale said quietly. "Since when have you been interested in people?"

Zarkov frowned. "But that's just it, Dale. It's Willie. He's got one of the finest scientific brains in the world. They wanted me to teach him everything I know about science. It was only when he came out here to the lab that I found out about his—"

"Where did you come from, Willie?" Flash asked, interrupting Zarkov.

"I'm an orphan," Willie said with a faint smile. "I've been going to school at the World Science Institute in Megalopolis West. That's where Dr. Zarkov found me." He ducked his head.

"You see," Zarkov boomed, "they thought Willie was an underachiever, because he paid no attention to his studies in school. But when they gave him an I.Q. test, he only missed two questions in two thousand. And so they wanted me to see him." Zarkov beamed. "I'm considered the greatest astrophysicist in the country, anyway, and it was only natural that they would send him to me for instruction."

Dale smiled wryly. "Naturally."

"And it was when Willie got here that I found out why he underachieved."

"Why was that?" Flash asked, looking at Willie.

Willie grinned.

"He's a dreamer," said Zarkov. "Because problems are so easy for him to solve, he simply spends most of his time daydreaming."

"But I don't understand yet about this psychokinesis

and extrasensory perception you were talking about in relation to him," Flash said, puzzled.

Zarkov settled back in a chair he had taken, motioning to Willie to be seated near them. "Willie doesn't know how it started, either," he explained. "But one day when he was daydreaming, Willie suddenly—" Zarkov broke off. "Why don't you tell them, Willie?"

Willie nodded, looking embarrassed. "The first time it happened, I was in school at the World Science Institute. I had finished the lesson, and was simply dreaming, looking out the window. I happened to see a mountain peak in the distance. I think it's called Old Baldy. And I wondered what it would be like up there on the top of the mountain. I kind of wished I was there," Willie said slowly. "And all of a sudden, there I was!"

Flash sat up straight. "You mean, you wished you were on top of the mountain, and suddenly you were?"

"Right," Willie said with a sheepish grin. "I was really there, too," he said, chuckling. "I walked around in the trees and brush and reached out and touched the ground. That kind of thing. I even pinched myself." He giggled. "Yeah, I was there."

"But then how did you get back?"

"I decided I had had enough of the mountain, and I kind of—well—I kind of let go of the idea, you know, and I was back in the classroom."

Flash looked at Zarkov. Zarkov laughed. "You see?"

"What about the classroom? Did anybody notice you were gone?"

"I don't think so. I guess that when I was gone I was still there," Willie said slowly. "Or maybe I imagined myself on the mountain in a split-second of time. You know?"

Flash nodded. "Sort of."

"Then I began to take more trips like that," said Willie.

"Did you tell anyone?" Dale asked.

"No," said Willie, ducking his head self-consciously. "Do you think I'm crazy? They'd all say I was nuts."

"I guess they would, at that," Flash said, laughing.

"Then when I came out here to the desert, I kind of imagined myself up on Black Hat Mountain one day, and there I was. Dr. Zarkov didn't even know I'd gone." He chuckled mischievously.

"But how did you find out about this power of Willie's, Doc?" Flash asked.

Zarkov smiled ruefully. "One day Willie and I were

working at the big telescopic mirror in the lab, jotting down notes on what we thought was a new quasar sighting, and—bingo!—suddenly we were both on another planet!"

Flash sat up straight.

"That's right," agreed Willie. "I just wished I was there with Doc."

"I'll be darned," Dale said wonderingly.

"But how did you get back?" Flash asked Zarkov.

"Willie finally let go of his idea, as he expresses it, and we were back here in the lab." Zarkov shook his head and pulled at his beard. "It was a scary moment or two, I'll tell you that! I made Willie promise never to do that to me again."

Willie laughed.

Dale looked up. "What's funny, Willie?"

"I can promise all I want, Miss Arden, but when I begin to imagine, it doesn't do any good. I go there—and so does Doc, now."

Zarkov tugged at his beard again. "That's why I sent for you two. Not only to let you meet Willie, but also to try to sit down with me and get Willie's power under control."

"You mean, work on the power with Willie until he can accurately determine how he manages to move himself and other people from one place to another?"

"Right," said Zarkov.

Flash turned to Willie. "How did you do that to us on the way out here, Willie? I mean in the car?"

Willie flushed and looked at the floor. "I was hungry, you know, but Doc wouldn't let me have a second dessert tonight. I was mad at him. And when I looked out the window and saw the headlights of your car coming across the desert, I suddenly thought dessert, and I imagined myself in a place where I could get all the dessert I wanted. The Big Rock Candy Mountain. And I was there, and then I wished you were there, too, because I had just seen your car coming toward the laboratory. And you were there, driving through the ice-cream sundaes and lollipops with me."

"We didn't see you," said Dale.

"No. I wished you wouldn't."

Flash shook his head. "It's a strange power, Willie. I don't know but that it's a very dangerous power."

"Not if it's used for good purposes Flash," Zarkov said firmly.

"Have you made tests with this thing?" Flash asked Zarkov.

"A few. But we haven't really started. That's what I wanted to consult with you about, Flash."

Flash nodded. "Right." He turned to Willie. "Willie, let me ask you a question—"

But suddenly Willie was not there at all, nor was the room, nor were Zarkov or Dale.

Flash rubbed his eyes.

He was standing in a very high, remote place, a kind of platform built out in empty air. And there, not ten feet away from him, down to one side, stood Worriless Willie, looking up at him.

"In a minute, Mr. Gordon."

Willie grinned. He bent over and scooped up a great handful of whipped cream, from what looked like a very large banana split, and began eating it.

"How is it, Willie?"

"I like it!" Willie grinned.

"You've done it again, haven't you?"

"Yes." Willie looked serious. "I didn't think you believed I could."

"I believe you, Willie," Flash said cautiously. "How do we get back to Doc's lab?"

"I guess you better just wait for me," Willie said, grinning. "If you try to get down from here, you may have a pretty long fall."

Flash peered over the edge of the platform and saw absolute, infinite space below him.

"Okay, Willie," he said, trying to keep his voice steady.

"I'll only be a second," said Willie, wiping the cream off his face.

Flash sighed and waited.

And waited.

Chapter 3

Dr. Zarkov's laughter boomed out through the room. "Now you know how I felt when I found myself with Willie on that silly planet. I didn't know how I got there or what happened."

Flash and Willie had returned suddenly from the place where Willie had dreamed up the banana split to find Zarkov and Dale chatting as if nothing had happened.

"Didn't you know we were gone?" Flash asked Dale in surprise.

"Sorry, no," Dale said, smiling.

"Well, we were gone," Flash responded sharply.

"I just didn't think about it," Dale admitted. "Did you, Doc?"

Zarkov frowned, closing his eyes to think back. "No. I can't really remember, but you did go with Willie?"

"Yes," Flash said, a bit annoyed that no one had missed him.

Willie grinned. "I won't do it again. I just wanted Mr. Gordon to know I could."

"And you wanted your miserable banana split," snapped Zarkov. "I don't know how you grow at all on the food you eat!"

They discussed Willie's power for several minutes more, but came to no conclusion as to how to harness or contain it.

And then Zarkov remembered the time he and Willie had "gone" to Mount Palomar when Zarkov had casually mentioned the famous observatory.

"How did you bet back?" Dale asked.

"I don't really know," Zarkov confessed. "One minute we were there, and then we were back at the telescope."

Willie spoke up. "I just wished we were back here and we were, Dr. Zarkov."

"I thought for a minute I was on Mongo again," Zarkov said darkly, "the time he sent us up to that fool planet. I can tell you that gave me a turn."

"Mongo?" Willie repeated, his green eyes lighting up.

"Yeah," said Zarkov. "That's where Flash and Dale and I first went by rocket years ago."

"Where's Mongo?" Willie asked.

"It passes through Earth's orbit every two and seven-tenths years. The first time it—"

"No, no," said Willie. "I mean where is it now?"

Flash frowned. "Due in about nine months. Right, Doc?"

Zarkov nodded. "Seems to me that's right. You've got to remember, Willie, that when Flash and I met Mongo was heading directly for Earth. On a collision course, as we say in the air force and navy."

Willie's eyes were wide. "What happened?"

Flash grinned. "It was pretty scary, Willie. I'm sure you've read about it."

"I never was any good at history. And you were there? Tell me how you felt. That's what I'd like to hear."

Flash scratched his head. "Well, I had just graduated from college, and Dale and I—"

"Flash," Dale said chidingly, "you're making it seem you were just anybody out of college! Willie, Flash was a star athlete while a student at Yale University. He was fencing champion and a great polo player, known all over the world. I met him at a polo tournament in England, in fact. I had gone there to visit my aunt. Then, when I returned to Megalopolis West, I found that Flash was working in the same company, Electronics Universal, that I was. And we started seeing each other."

"Gee," said Willie. "That's interesting, but what about the darned planet? Mongo, I mean, headed for earth?"

"That's just it. Scientists at Mount Palomar had first seen the planet coming into our solar system several days before."

"Yes," Flash said, "the planet had somehow spun off from the gravitational field of the Mongo system and was headed into ours. It looked at first as if it would hit earth head-on."

"It was a very trying time," Dale said. "Flash and I were both sent by Electronics Universal to Washington to attend an important meeting with the secretary of state and the ambassadors from many European countries. We were flying in an eastbound transcontinental plane when it happened."

"What happened?" Willie asked, his eyes wide.

"A piece of flaming meteor had entered earth's atmosphere," Flash explained. "It had, in fact, been torn off from Mongo, apparently when Mongo had been wrenched out of its own solar system. When the meteor shot through our thicker atmospheric system from space, it caught fire and slammed toward earth. The pilot of the plane we were on tried to veer to one side, but the meteor caught the tip of the port wing and ripped it off."

"Golly!" Willie exclaimed. "What did you do?"

"The plane was hopelessly disabled and began to spin out of control," Flash explained. "In those days, there were parachutes stored in the companionway for emergencies and the entire group of us on board the ship bailed out. I grabbed Dale and the two of us were the last out. Moments after we had left the ship, it plummeted to earth, where it exploded in a holocaust of fire."

"Yipes!" Willie said. "And you?"

"We were caught in a hot updraft from the fire on the desert and blown many miles from the site of the wreck. And we came down not far from the very spot where we are now."

"I'll be darned!" Willie said. "Here at Dr. Zarkov's laboratory?"

"Exactly," said Flash. "And he was the first person we saw after we landed."

"Did he help you?" asked Willie.

Flash snorted. "Not likely! He ran out of his laboratory and confronted us with a gun. He said he was going to kill us."

"Wow!"

Zarkov growled in his throat. "You're making me sound like some kind of maniac," he said irritably.

"Which you were," Dale said, cutting in.

"Perhaps, but there was a reason for it."

Flash grinned. "There was, Doc. You tell it."

"Willie, I'd been working day and night, ever since the runaway planet was discovered by the scientists at Mount Palomar, to perfect a rocket in my underground laboratory here. The work, incidentally, was financed by a big foundation located in Megalopolis East."

Willie's eyes were wide. "That was before they had rocket travel, wasn't it?"

"You bet it was. I had been working on this theory for years, but the war had made me go underground with my prototypes, for fear the enemy might conspire to steal my thrust formulas. They were the crux of the entire model."

"Gee!" Willie said gasping. "And so you were trying to perfect your rocket and—"

"I had perfected it," Zarkov said proudly. "But I had been so security-conscious that I became unnerved when Flash and Dale appeared, more or less right out of the sky. I thought they were enemies of America. I thought they might be spies sent to kill me and make off with the rocket, or saboteurs who would destroy my prototype."

"Doc was really off his rocker," Flash said with a smile.

"He was crackers," Dale said, shaking her head at the memory of the disheveled, wild-eyed man who had confronted them that dark and dreadful night.

"I told them they would have to come with me," Zarkov continued, "that I wouldn't kill them if they did, because I didn't want to waste the bullets in my gun. I wanted them to help me. And they came aboard all right."

Flash shook his head. "Doc isn't telling this very well. He forced us aboard the rocket, which he had loaded with the most powerful explosives known to man at that time. It was Zarkov's idea that he could direct the rocket toward the approaching planet, which we came later to discover was Mongo, and simply blow it off its course toward Earth by crash-landing there."

"Son of a gun, Willie cried admiringly. "You mean, more or less intercept the planet, and divert it from its collision course with Earth?"

"That's it," said Dale.

"What happened?" Willie asked.

"Dale and I more or less accepted our fate and joined Zarkov aboard the rocket. We thought that we would help him, even though he was unhinged. It would be a noble sacrifice to save the Earth we loved."

Willie nodded. "Yeah," he whispered. "That's good."

"So we helped him get the rocket ready, we climbed aboard, sealed the hatches, and blasted off."

"But how did you live through the explosion when the rocket hit Mongo?" Willie asked, frowning.

Flash smiled. "Actually, Doc's rocket was very well constructed, but when it came into Mongo's atmosphere he found that he was not able to control it. The gravitational pull was slightly less than Earth's and Doc's finely tuned guidance system was off enough to make the matter serious."

Zarkov nodded ruefully. "The system was too perfect. If it hadn't been so good, it would have worked on Mongo, too."

Flash laughed. "Doc, admit it. You've had more crash landings than anyone in space. This was just the first."

Zarkov shrugged. "Get on with the story, Flash."

"Okay, then. That's it—the rocket crash-landed because Doc couldn't guide it correctly in the different gravitational field."

"What happened?" Willie gasped.

"Well, we went into the Sea of Mystery, right next to Mingo City. The explosives didn't go off."

"Mingo City? Where's that?"

"It's part of the inhabited section of Mongo, Willie."

"How about that? But Mr. Gordon—what about the planet?"

"What about Mongo?"

"If the explosives didn't go off, how come the planet didn't hit earth? And how did you keep from drowning in the Sea of Mystery?"

"The explosives didn't count at all. We never knew all this until later, but the scientists on Mongo were far more advanced than we were on Earth. They had already set up an electric force, a sort of antigravity shield around their whole planet, and the planet passed near the Earth but never struck it."

"Gee!"

"But by the time we found out what had happened, Mongo and Earth were again far apart and there we were, stranded in a strange world."

"But what about the Sea of Mystery? How come you didn't drown?"

Flash smiled. "We got out before the rocket had plunged too deeply into the water, and swam to shore. We were plenty lucky we didn't land far out at sea. And we immediately became involved with Ming the Merciless's coast guard. It was a touchy thing, Willie."

"Holy smoke! Tell me about, Mr. Gordon."

Flash glanced at Zarkov. "What about it, Doc? Isn't it time for Willie to be in bed?"

Zarkov frowned. "Well, maybe you can tell him a little bit about Mongo. The Lion Men. The Hawkmen. Ming's armies. And maybe Queen Azura, the Witch Queen of Mongo."

"Especially her," Dale said sarcastically.

"I always did favor that girl," Zarkov boomed good-naturedly.

"So did Flash," snapped Dale, her face set.

"I did not," Flash countered. "Dale, you never will understand that adventure of mine, will you?"

"Gee, Mr. Gordon, tell me what you're talking about, will you?"

Flash glanced at Dale, then back to Zarkov. He sighed. "Okay, Willie. Just a few more minutes, and then you're headed for bed."

Chapter 4

Forty-five minutes later, Flash stopped talking. Willie was staring at him, wide-eyed and completely absorbed in the adventures of long ago.

"Mr. Gordon," he said breathlessly, "after you were stranded on the planet Mongo, did it still run wild through the universe?"

"No," Flash answered.

"Why not?"

"The planet had lost momentum. Finally, the effects of our own sun overcame its swing through space and it pulled Mongo into a gravitational orbit around our own sun."

"I guess I did read that somewhere," Willie said.

"Mongo now travels in a rather strange orbit in our own solar system for part of its orbit, but goes around its own sun for the other part."

"I see."

"Several years after we crashed there," Flash said, "Mongo crossed the asteriod belt, and Dale and Doc and I were able to make a rocket flight back to Earth."

"Great!" said Willie.

Dale spoke up. "It's been about six years since we returned to Earth, hasn't it, Flash?"

Flash nodded.

Willie frowned, turning his head slightly. "Hey, Dr. Zarkov, isn't something making a noise in your laboratory?"

Zarkov cocked his head. "You're right, Willie. Some kind of buzzing. It sounds like a signal from the space-scanner."

Flash stood up. "Let's have a look, shall we?"

Zarkov was halfway to the door of the lab.

Dale rose, and they all went into the high-ceilinged observatory next to the lab.

The observatory was dominated by the large electronic telescope stationed right in the center, with green radar-screens of all shapes and sizes spaced out around the large mirror.

Zarkov waved his hand about. "These receivers are tuned in to a statellite cruising in the upper atmosphere. The instruments on the satellite flash a signal when they pick up unusual disturbances out there."

"Wow!" Willie said, peering into one of the scanner screens. "Can you tell what you've spotted?"

"Sometimes." Zarkov peered toward one large screen and adjusted a series of dials on the console's face. The green shimmering indistinctness suddenly focused brightly and a clear picture emerged.

"There!" Willie cried.

Flash peered forward. "It's a planet, Doc." He frowned. "Doesn't look like any of ours. Hey—!"

Zarkov was excited. "How about that—it's Mongo. And how coincidental, when we were just talking about it. Must be that Mongo has settled into a new kind of orbit and is coming around sooner than two and seven-tenths years."

"Hey, look!" cried Willie. "It seems to be headed right for Earth again."

"It's just an illusion," Flash said. "But it'll be at its closest now for the next two and seven-tenths years."

Willie waved his arms excitedly. "Gee, Mr. Gordon, this may be our chance. You could take us through space to Mongo and we could see the Lion Men and the Hawkmen and the Tree Kingdom of Arboria."

"Hold it there, Willie," Flash said, laughing. "I've got friends on Mongo I'd like to visit, but planets travel at incredible speeds. When Mongo's close by, we could get there in a few days, but a week after it passes Earth it would take months to get back."

"Would it?" Willie asked, suddenly very quiet.

Zarkov turned quickly from the scanner and stared at Willie. "Willie!" he cried. "No—you wouldn't!"

"Willie," yelled Flash. "You don't know what you're doing."

"Yes, I do," said Willie.

And he did.

Chapter 5

They stood on an outcropping of shalelike rock in a strange and exotic land: the planet of Mongo.

Purplish mountains rose in the distance, silhouetted against the slightly tawny atmosphere of the planet. Nearer to them a series of small lemon-colored foothills rolled across the long prairie. The flat plain was covered with an ankle-height growth of Mongoturf, a weed that was prevalent throughout the planet, with several gnarled trees resembling Earth's oak scattered here and there. Many of the "oak" were dead.

Between the foothills and the point where they stood, a stream of dirty brown water trickled along over shining green boulders.

"Oceanite," Zarkov muttered, still annoyed by Worriless Willie's impulsiveness.

"What's oceanite?" Flash asked irritably.

"Rock formation," Zarkov said, tugging at his beard.

"I don't care about the rock formation," snapped Dale. "How did we get here? And how do we get away?"

Flash turned to Willie. "Well? Now, how about thinking us a return trip to Earth."

Willie smiled slightly and looked at the ground. Then he scuffed his feet a bit. Finally, he looked up slyly at Flash.

"I don't know, Mr. Gordon. Now that we're here, I guess it wouldn't hurt any to just sort of look around, would it? Just for a little glance at this historic place?"

Flash's eyes narrowed. "I thought so. What you're saying is that your thinking trick won't work unless you want it to. Is that right?"

"That's right," Willie said.

"And you don't want it to, do you?"

"No," Willie admitted.

Dale reached out and took Willie's shoulders and shook them. "Willie! This is no place for us to be. It's dangerous. Flash and Dr. Zarkov and I were almost killed here the first time we landed. There are all sorts of wild beasts and—"

"I don't see any," Willie answered, smiling and looking around.

Flash shook his head. "Forget it, Dale. If Willie insists, I suppose we've got to look around, as he says, for a little bit."

Zarkov had been staring at the purplish mountains in the distance.

"You know, I can't quite tell exactly where we are, Flash, but those mountains look familiar."

"Familiar?" Dale asked.

"I can't place them. It's been six years since I was here." Zarkov tugged at his beard. "Damn, I wish we had some kind of spacecraft. We could cruise around and get the lay of the land."

Willie grinned. "Let's just walk awhile, huh? How about that?"

Flash put his hand on Willie's shoulder. "Listen to me, Willie. I'm not going to bawl you out for what you did. It wouldn't do any good, and besides that it wouldn't make you like me anymore than you already do. But I want to tell you one thing."

"What's that, Mr. Gordon?"

"There's no way of telling where you have located us on the planet of Mongo. We may be in friendly territory or we may be in unfriendly territory. We've simply got to find out, and find out now—or get out immediately. How about it, Willie?"

There was a long silence.

"No," Willie said finally, after a few moments' thought. "I want to stay awhile. Mr. Gordon, I've never had any adventures like you. I've never been in a strange land before. I've never seen weird rocks and funny trees and shining green boulders, and all that."

Flash shrugged.

"So I want to stay. If it's unfriendly territory, well, I guess you and Dr. Zarkov can do something about protecting us, can't you?"

Zarkov raised his fists into the air and shook them helplessly. "You're not making my day, Willie," he cried. "You know that?"

Willie nodded. "I know, Dr. Zarkov, but it's the way I feel. You told me always to be honest and I'm being honest. I want to see some of Mongo, no matter how dangerous it is. A man has to meet danger head-on, doesn't he?"

"Well, Willie," Zarkov said slowly.

"You told me that yourself, Dr. Zarkov."

Zarkov threw back his head and closed his eyes as his lips moved silently. "I'm counting to ten, Willie. When I get through, I want to see us back in the desert outside Megalopolis West."

There was a short silence.

Zarkov opened his eyes. "Willie?"

"No, Dr. Zarkov," Willie said softly.

Zarkov's hands slapped his thighs in resignation. "So be it. Then come on—we've got to do some exploring to find out where we are."

Flash stared at Willie, glanced at Dale, and then turned from them. "There's no sign of a city anywhere around here. I think we'd better get up onto high ground and have a look there."

"Right," said Dale. "Let's go."

"I think we're somewhere in the Volcano World," mused Zarkov as they walked along the rocky formation toward the foothills in the distance.

"That would put us east of the Great Mongo Jungle, and also of Arboria," Flash said decisively.

Dale frowned. "But doesn't that mean we'd have to cross the Great Mongo Desert to get to Arboria?"

"I'm afraid so," Flash said. He hesitated. "Actually, we may be north of the Great Mongo Desert and in Arboria Territory, in which case we need not worry. No one would attack us there."

"We'll have to find out from one of these high peaks," Zarkov said wearily. "Willie, are you sure you don't wish to go back to Earth yet?"

Willie looked about him with exhilaration. "I'm sure, Dr. Zarkov."

Zarkov sighed. "I never did understand teenagers."

"It's the generation gap," Willie said laughing.

They continued their walk in the clear air of Mongo.

"Hey," Willie said, "you know, it's easier to breathe here than on Earth."

"No pollution," said Zarkov. "If we had any sense on Earth, we wouldn't have allowed the atmosphere to become so fouled up."

"Then why don't we do something about it?" Willie wondered.

"Maybe you could wish it clean," Dale suggested with a chuckle.

"I don't think it would work," Willie said seriously.

Zarkov boomed out: "We could always try. That is, when we get back to Earth." He paused dramatically. "If we get back."

Willie looked hurt. "Dr. Zarkov, you're making me feel awful. I just want to look around a little bit more. You people have been here before; this is my first trip. I haven't even seen a Mongo person yet."

"Luckily we haven't run across any followers of Ming the Merciless."

"Is Ming the Merciless still alive?" Willie asked excitedly.

"No," said Flash. "He was killed when Prince Barin defeated Mingo and stabilized the government of the entire planet in the Free Council of Mongo."

"Then why should we worry about anyone from Mingo?" Willie wondered.

"Actually, we shouldn't," Flash admitted. "It's just that Doc and I remember the way it used to be when we were always fighting Ming the Merciless's armies—to the death."

Zarkov had stopped in his tracks. "We're at a fork in the trace," he said.

Flash looked ahead. The trail split and one branch went to the left and the other to the right. The left road twisted back and forth toward the top of a peak with an orange cast to it. The other road went up the peak to the right, which was a bluish color.

"We've got to split up, Doc," said Flash. "You take the left road; I'll take the right."

"Okay," said Zarkov. "Come on, Willie."

Willie frowned. "I want to go to the right with Mr. Gordon."

Flash shook his head. "I'd better take Dale, Willie. Why don't you go with Doc?"

Dale put her hand on Flash's arm. "That's okay, Flash. Take Willie with you. Doc and I will be all right."

"I know you'll be all right," Flash said, "but—" then he sighed. "All right. Come on, Willie. Let's go."

Zarkov and Dale waved to them and started off up the left-hand fork. After a moment, Flash and Willie took the right one.

Within a half hour, they were completely out of sight of the foothills and the plain behind them were winding up amidst great formations of a bluish crystalline rock. The crystal stalagmites were so high and pointed that the saffron atmosphere of Mongo was almost obscured by them. The sunlight reflected off them in shimmering blazes of blue light, with the trail rising ever more steeply toward the summit of the mountain.

"We should be coming to the top soon," Flash said. "Then we can look out and see what lies to the right of us; I hope we were not mistaken and it's Prince Barin's land."

Willie smiled. "It's terrific, hiking like this in a strange land, Mr. Gordon."

Flash smiled faintly. "I'm glad you like it, Willie. I'm trying to forget that it's because of you we're doing this."

"I'll never forget you for it, Mr. Gordon," said Willie. "You've been real good to me to do this for me."

Flash stepped around a tall spike of bluish crystal and came to a narrow stretch of passageway between two high, steep cliffs of the dark-blue rock. It was at least a thousand feet to the top of the cliffs. The pathway went straight ahead and then turned sharply to the right.

A rock hurtling from above suddenly slammed into the path not ten feet in front of them. Flash glanced up the steep cliff faces. He saw nothing up there.

"What was that?" Willie asked. His voice sounded shaky.

"Nothing," said Flash. "Just a rock. It must have become dislodged from the cliff and fallen in front of us."

Willie looked around furtively. "Maybe. You know, Mr. Gordon, it's kind of spooky here."

Flash turned to him with amusement. "Ready to go home, Willie?"

Willie shook his head emphatically and looked away. "Not yet, Mr. Gordon."

Flash chuckled. "What's the matter? Do you think someone's watching us?"

Willie nodded. "I do, Mr. Gordon."

"So do I," Flash admitted, and then turned to move on. "Well, whoever it is, I hope they get their eyes filled. Come on."

They marched along through the narrow passageway, turned to the right, and came out on a narrow, wedge-shaped ledge that overlooked a sharp cliff that dropped off into nothingness directly in front of them. In the distance, Flash saw a vast, blue, shimmering haze that covered the whole landscape, shrouding it from sight.

He knew instantly where he was.

And at the same moment, Willie screamed.

"Mr. Gordon! Look!"

Flash wheeled. Willie was pointing to a pile of boulders beside the pathway, over which three figures were climbing. The figures wore hoods and brilliant electric-blue robes, tied with a golden chain at the waist. Their faces were invisible inside the dark hoods, wreathed as they were in some kind of blue gauze, but Flash could discern gleaming eyes and bright teeth behind the drawn-back lips.

"An ambush," snapped Flash. "And we've got no weapons."

The first hooded figure slipped its right hand into its cloak and drew out a long-handled ax, the blade composed of a kind of bluish steel. The curved head, with sharp points at the ends, was fitted over a wooden handle, with the rear end of the blade protruding as a sharply curved point. It resembled an old-fashioned, highly stylized, adz.

"Run for it!" cried Flash. "I'll hold them off!"

A second hooded figure reached out, leaped over the boulder in front of Flash, and grabbed Willie before he could move, holding him motionless against the rock cliff.

The leading figure jumped at Flash, wielding the ax in his hand.

The third stood on top of the rocks, watching with sardonic amusement.

Flash tensed his muscles, ready to jump.

"Ouch!" screamed Willie. "You're hurting me!"

Flash wheeled. The second figure was throttling Willie by the throat and Willie's face was red from the struggles. He could hardly breathe.

Flash changed his mind and dove for the hooded figure holding Willie. The leading figure raised his hand and an ax sailed through the air directly at Flash's neck.

Chapter 6

Worriless Willie was definitely a dreamer. His mind had a habit of wandering about and paying no attention to things that went on near him. In school, the teachers had always accused him of sleeping when he was awake.

They were wrong. Willie simply had a great imagination. He liked to think about wonderful things and imagine he was there where the wonderful things were happening.

At least, it had been that way at first. He had thought about great things happening and he had imagined he was there. Then, about two years ago, he had discovered to his surprise and delight that when he thought about some other place where wonderful things were happening, he suddenly was able to travel through space instantly, using only his mind to propel him.

And Willie had turned into something other than a dreamer. He had become a mystery and an object of astonishment and wonderment to his teachers and the kids at the orphanage.

There was something a little bit annoying about it all, really. It seemed that everyone wanted Willie to use his imagination all the time to propel himself and them through space to other worlds and places, so they could write it down in a magazine, or turn it into a scientific monograph.

Willie had just about had it with all that guff.

Once they got back to Earth, he was going to talk to Dr. Zarkov about it. No more experiments with Willie. Willie wanted to go back to his friends and be the way he was before he imagined himself into a scientific oddity.

It was with a feeling of real shock that Willie suddenly realized that his mind had been wandering once again. He was daydreaming, as they used to tell him in school.

And what was happening right next to him was utterly terrifying.

He had to get out of this place immediately! He was in danger.

He opened his eyes and felt the world turning swiftly under him. And instantly he remembered where he was and what was happening. It was a rude awakening to Willie, coming out of a beautiful dream and finding reality stark and cold and terrible right there in front of his eyes.

The hooded figure had him around the throat, squeezing him and cutting off the air from his chest. Willie saw small black dots dance in front of his eyes, and his vision suddenly began to go red. He knew he was on the brink of losing consciousness. He had lost consciousness once before, when he had been very tired after running around the track because he had not eaten enough beforehand. He knew what that was like.

He could feel the black waves breaking over him now, like combers at the beach.

He knew what to do. He would think himself back to Dr. Zarkov's lab.

He did so.

And there he was—in the laboratory, looking out across the darkened desert. He turned. Where were the others?

Then he realized that none of the rest were there with him. Somehow he had not thought enough about them to bring them with him. He had been incredibly and inexcusably selfish in wishing only himself safe from danger.

Beside that, Dr. Zarkov had not been with him when he and Mr. Gordon were captured by the hooded figures. He could not wish him and Miss Arden back with the two of them.

How could he leave Dr. Zarkov and Miss Arden on Mongo like that? And Mr. Gordon?

He did not want to go back to that hooded figure with the strong hands, either, but he knew he had to. It was a duty, more or less. After all, it was because of Willie that Dr. Zarkov and Mr. Gordon were on Mongo. And he had said he wanted to stay around and look the planet over.

The rest of them had wanted to go home.

He had made the decision. He could not cop out on it this way, and leave the rest of them stranded there, helpless—and Mr. Gordon about to be split down the middle with the ax Willie had seen the hooded man throw.

No, he would have to return and see what he could do about it.

And he was back, the air squeezed out of his chest, his vision blurring, and the sound of heavy breathing in his ears.

Stop! he thought. Stop!

Immediately, the hooded figure who was strangling him froze.

Willie opened his eyes, trying to see what had happened. He had thought Stop!, but he did not know what he had actually caused to happen.

He saw Flash Gordon frozen in position, waiting for the ax to hit him. He saw the ax frozen in the air. He saw the two other hooded figures standing like statues in exactly the position they had been in when he thought Stop!

Willie scrambled out of the tight grasp of the hooded man and fell to the ground. He crawled up onto his knees and stared about him.

Yes, he had stopped time. He had frozen them all in time: people, objects, and the planet of Mongo itself.

It was simply one more aspect of his astonishing power. He smiled brightly.

"I did it," he cried out. "I did it!"

But this wasn't helping Mr. Gordon at all. He stared at Flash Gordon, wondering what to do about him. Then it came to him. He simply willed Flash Gordon to continue to do what he had been doing.

Flash ducked involuntarily, as he had been going to do at the first glimpse of the ax flying toward him. Now he stared at the ax frozen in flight, and then his eyes turned to Willie incredulously.

"Willie," he said. "How did you do that?"

Willie ducked his head. "I just kind of imagined it, Mr. Gordon."

Flash smiled faintly. "You saved my life, Willie."

"Saved my own, too," Willie said with a grin.

"I'd guess by looking around us that you can make time stand still, Willie."

"I guess so, Mr. Gordon."

"It was very brave of you, Willie, to save my life that way."

Willie thought about the way he had really thought

first only of himself, and had imagined himself back in the safety of Dr. Zarkov's lab, and he was ashamed.

"Well, I really guess I wasn't so brave, Mr. Gordon."

Flash frowned.

"I just imagined myself home, first of all, and didn't think about anybody else at all."

Flash put his hand on Willie's shoulder. "But you did come back to help me, Willie," he said kindly.

Willie felt his face turn red. "Yes, sir."

"And that's what counts."

Willie felt warm and happy suddenly. He turned toward the hooded figure who had been strangling him. "What'll we do now, Mr. Gordon?"

Flash looked at the three hooded men and walked over to the one who still held an ax. He pulled it out of the man's hand and held it for a moment.

"It looks like some kind of ancient adz," he said musingly. "Must be out of an era equivalent to Earth's Iron Age." He frowned. "Still those hoods and robes look familiar to me in a strange way."

"Do you know these people?" Willie asked.

Flash shook his head briefly. "I don't think so, Willie. It's hard to tell. Still, they might be. . . ." Flash shook his head finally.

He reached out and pulled the second ax from the air, and then helped Willie pull the concealed ax from the third hooded figure's robe. The two of them walked over to the edge of the rocky cliff and threw the three weapons over.

Flash turned to Willie and winked.

"Guess that evens things up a bit. Now we can go at it again."

Willie nodded. "You sure you don't want to leave them here, Mr. Gordon?"

Flash grinned. "Never leave a job unfinished, Willie. Remember that." He rubbed his hands together and stood waiting for Willie to unfreeze time.

Willie closed his eyes and thought, Go!

The hooded figure who had been shaking Willie turned quickly in surprise, and reached out for Willie where he now stood, but Willie was waiting for him and ducked. When the hooded figure stumbled past him, Willie reached out, grabbed his booted leg, and flipped up hard.

The hooded figure crashed into the flat stone cliff by the pathway and slumped to the ground.

Flash, in turn, jumped toward the hooded figure who had thrown the ax at him. The hooded man, surprised to see that the ax had vanished before his eyes, was momentarily taken off-guard.

Driving hard with his legs, Flash grabbed him around the waist in a football tackle and pushed him toward the edge of the cliff. The hooded figure cried out in terror, looking back over his shoulder.

The two of them fell struggling onto the ground, and Flash quickly subdued him by pulling his arm into a tight hammerlock.

"Look out!" cried Willie.

Flash turned just as the third attacker loomed over him, ready to strike him with a rock. Quickly, Flash kicked out and lashed the hooded man across the upper thigh. He screamed and twisted aside. The rock fell harmlessly to the ground.

With a curling motion, Flash rose and grabbed the man around the shoulders, bearing him to the ground. The hooded figure threw Flash off, and Flash gave him a quick karate chop to the neck.

The third man went down.

Flash stood and grinned at Willie.

"Gee, that was great, Mr. Gordon! What are we going to do now?"

Flash considered. "I've got a hunch about where these hatchetmen come from."

"Where, Mr. Gordon?" Willie asked, his eyes wide with excitement.

"Never mind," said Flash. "I think it means trouble, though. I think we'd better go look for Doc and Dale."

Flash was staring about him carefully.

Willie walked over to the edge of the cliff and looked over. It seemed miles down to the bottom of the drop. Willie blinked.

"It's a long drop!"

Flash joined him. "That's right, Willie."

"Hey, Mr. Gordon," Willie said suddenly. "Look." He pointed past a group of boulders where the three hooded figures had first attacked them. In the rock face behind them was an opening like the mouth of a cave.

Flash peered past the rocks. "It's a cave."

"Yeah," Willie said, taking a deep breath. "And it's

really creepy-looking, isn't it?" He was studying the blue rock around the cave mouth, and the shimmer of stalactites and stalagmites dimly seen inside the blue mistiness of the cavern beyond.

Flash nodded grimly. "Yes, it is that, Willie. And now I do know where we are. We've got to get back to Doc and Dale before it's too late."

"Too late?"

"Yes. If I'm not mistaken, that entrance leads to the Kingdom of Blue Magic."

"Wow!" Willie said. "The Kingdom of Blue Magic. Why don't we go there, Mr. Gordon? Why don't we go inside the cave and take a good look around?"

"No, Willie. We've got to make tracks out of here, and get Doc and Dale."

"Look!" cried Willie. "There's something coming out of the cave mouth. It's a kind of mist."

Flash peered ahead. The mist was rolling slowly and majestically from the mouth of the cave, coming right up over the rocks and into their eyes.

Willie smelled a very faint perfume, a delightful smell, like some kind of spicy shaving lotion.

Flash started to speak.

"Willie, we've got to get away from this stuff. It's—"

Willie turned. He saw Flash staring at him, mouth open, unable to utter a sound. And Willie realized that he could not move a muscle of his own body.

He was powerless.

The blue haze surrounded the two of them, wrapping them in its tentacles and then rising all around them to cover them like a shroud.

Willie could not imagine himself away this time because even his willpower was taken from him.

Chapter 7

Deep within the inner core of the planet Mongo were located the subterranean caverns of a strange and sunless world—Azuria, the Kingdom of Blue Magic. When Mongo's crust had first formed many millions of years ago, subterranean gasses had erupted, blowing out mountains and hills among the oceans and seas that had formerly made up the entire surface of the planet.

A great part of the core of Mongo had been formed of a type of petroleum mass similar to Earth's oil, and it was this enormous deposit that had caught on fire during the eruptive process of the planet and burned out through the vents and fissures caused by the eruption of the volcanic pustules.

Eventually this enormous inner conflagration had burned itself out, leaving a tremendous area in the middle of the planet without any sign of vegetation or life even though it was all empty space. The giant chamber was reached through the vents and fissures caused by escaping gasses from the fire that had formed the inner endoglobe, called the Caverna Gigantea by scientists when it was discovered.

Sunlight penetrated the inner chambers of this vast area only in refracted or re-refracted rays, which made their way to the inside with only a trace of their original illumination intact. What remained was a strange bluish glow more like the dying dot of light on a vidscreen than a diminished ray of sunlight.

The geologic formation that encased this strange Caverna Gigantea was a type of rock existent only on Mongo, called oceanite for its bluish color. The lode of oceanite extended all the way from the center of the planet to the small chain of mountains that was upthrust in the middle of the Great Mongo Desert, the land that separated Arboria, the Kingdom of Prince Barin, and the Volcano World and Jungle of Barbaran.

It was in the middle of the Caverna Gigantea, the absolute dead center of the planet of Mongo, that an enormous jeweled city had been built by the first members of the Azurian race. The Azurians were named for the indigo-pigmented skins, which had resulted from an early cataclysmic scientific experiment controlled by the scientific council of the People of the Desert, as the Azurians were called before their mutation, who had been trying to revitalize the Great Mongo Desert for colonization.

The experiment had been subverted by a group of power-mad scientists in the pay of a would-be dictator whose name has been lost in the annals of Mongo. After altering the reclamation project into a vast nerve gas and biological-warfare department—all quite secret from the leaders of the planet—the scientific cabal had invented the perfect nerve gas along with its antidote.

The project had been discovered, however, and when the scientific cabal had turned the newly perfected nerve gas on the security people who had come to close the project down, the entire population had been afflicted and put to sleep.

Later, when the effects of the gas had worn off, the People of the Desert awoke to find themselves changed in appearance from a tanned outdoor color to a very light-intensity indigo which could not stand the direct rays of the sun.

It was assumed that the indigo color in the pigmentation of their skins had come from the mineral oceanite used in the formulation of the nerve gas.

After putting the scientists to death, the People of the Desert, now calling themselves Azurians after the color of their tinted skins, had hidden from the sun for years in subterranean abodes dug deep in the sand and rock of the Great Mongo Desert. Then, when one of their adventuresome tribe discovered the caves in the great chamber beneath the surface of Mongo, the Caverna Gigantea, they had migrated there and built an enormous city in the middle of the planet's endoglobe.

But science was still the favorite pastime of the Azurians. Inside the planet's core their most intelligent practitioners continued to perform their scientific experiments, inventing drugs and potions of all kinds, and building luxuries for their beautiful jeweled homes.

They learned to make stone of great beauty out of desert minerals; they learned to make pills that contained all the nourishment of the universe; they learned to make vapors and gasses that kept them young and vigorous forever. For that reason the country of Azuria became known as the Kingdom of the Blue Magic, with penetration into the secret area tantamount to sudden death for any trespasser.

In the winding walkways of the fantastically beautiful palace of Azuria strolled a statuesque and bounteously endowed black-haired woman of extreme physical beauty. She wore a band of platinum inset with beryl, turquoise, and sapphire, which gave off brilliant facets of light in the subdued bluish vapor that swirled throughout the Caverna Gigantea.

She wore a filmy lavendar cape on her bare back, clasped together at her throat with a chain of the finest gold and silver. Her garment covered her upper body in a tight, contoured sheath, clinging to her waist and hips with a luminescent glitter. Shoulder-length gloves of the same material covered each of her lovely arms and her feet were clad in tiny sea-blue sandals.

Queen Azura was deep in thought. Lines of care, not usually on her forehead, marred the singular beauty of her face only to a minor degree as she continued to mull over the latest news she had received from her secret agents working in Arboria.

"So," she said to herself as she walked along, "Prince Barin thinks he can seal off the tunnels to the xanthillium mines, does he? I've made up my mind about him. He and the Free Council of Mongo will rue the day they forced me to take action against them."

Queen Azura did not realize she was speaking out loud. She had been worrying about the xanthillium supply for months now, knowing that Prince Barin would eventually put a stop to Azuria's raids on the mineral. Xanthillium was a jellowing element peculiar to Mongo which, mixed with oceanite, formed duraplast, an almost indestructible metal equivalent to steel in strength and only one tenth its weight.

But all the xanthillium on Mongo was located in an enormous lode under the forest of Arboria in Prince

Barin's territory. For years Queen Azura's miners had worked from the subterranean vaults dug by past dynasties to bring xanthillium down into Azuria, the Kingdom of Blue Magic, but Prince Barin had finally discovered the pilferage and had brought the matter before the Free Council of Mongo.

Naturally, the Free Council had debated the case with Azuria's representative, a half-breed who could stand the sun's rays, arguing for Queen Azura. And just as naturally, the Grand Council had decided to forbid Queen Azura's miners from pulling out any more xanthillium.

Prince Barin had sought to enforce the ruling.

With Azuria and Arboria living almost side by side in a state of uneasy equilibrium, the tension had mounted, and Queen Azura's secret agents had made forays at night into the City of Wood—all of which had not pleased Prince Barin in the least.

In fact, the entire matter of xanthillium and mining rights was but the tip of the iceberg as far as Queen Azura was concerned. For years she had been working on a scheme to bring down the government of the Free Council of Mongo by sending her soldiers against Arboria and the nations allied with Arboria. And that scheme, she was happy to realize, waited only for one final element to bring it into play. A catalyst was the term her war minister used. A catalyst to force a showdown between the troops of Azuria and Arboria.

Just today, she had heard from one of her agents that Prince Barin was mounting an army of security troops to patrol the area of the mine, particularly the fissures in the planet's crust through which Azurian geologists took out the xanthillium.

This might be the catalyst, Azura knew, and yet she did not quite like the thrust of events. The catalyst should give her side extra leverage, so the war that would be precipitated would be to her advantage, not the opposition's.

It was a perplexing problem. Yet the right time might never come. Perhaps it was the hour—the do-or-die day!

"All right," Queen Azura said finally. "I've made up my mind. I'll do it, using him, and Prince Barin has only himself to blame!"

"Him," an exiled personage whom she had been hiding for years in the kingdom for just this purpose, was an unknown quantity, and a potential danger whom she had never really been able to completely master or even analyze. She was reluctant to use him, but. . . .

She turned on her heel and started to hurry back to the glittering entrance to the palace. She was startled to find she was not alone in the crushed-rock walkway that led through the garden of mineral formations.

"Qilp!" she exclaimed, frowning. "What are you doing on this forbidden pathway?"

The walkways around the palace were taboo to commoners. Qilp was minister of intelligence, but he was not of royal blood. He did not seem to be concerned at his trespass. There was great excitement on his face.

"Your Majesty!" he cried, his squeaky voice high and resonant in his throat. "We've got something on the scanner!"

Queen Azura stared at Qilp. He was only four feet high, his head just above her waist. The skull was enormous, with no hair growing on it at all. He had light-blue skin, with electric-blue eyes and strange teeth that seemed translucent. His neck was the size of a rope, and his arms and legs were thin and bony. He wore a body stocking of indigo from his neck to his knees, and on his abnormally large feet he wore flat sandals of plastic alloy.

"Go back to the palace," said Queen Azura. Scanner! He was using scientific terms again. Azuria's scanner was an ancient one, leftover from the early days of Azuria's existence on Mongo. While the latest scanners in use aboveground on the planet were of the vacuum-tube variety, the early ones were simple crystalline globular formations. Actually, the crystalline formulation caught vid-impulses perfectly and were not always in need of repair or replacement. But the vacuum tube had replaced the crystalline globules for all practical purposes.

But to Queen Azura, it was much more in keeping with the magic of the Kingdom of Blue Magic to call the scanner a crystal ball, rather than to admit it was simply a scientific device like everything else in the kingdom.

Qilp scampered for the door, his enormous feet splaying out and scattering crushed blue stones in all directions. Azura passed the bubbling fountain that sprayed blue water down over stalagmites of orange, green, and yellow, and finally reached the door to the palace.

In moments, she was inside the "I" Chamber of the palace. "I" for "eye," she told everyone. In actuality, it was "I" for "Intelligence."

The crystal sat on a stand in the corner of the room. When Azura entered, she found she was alone except for Qilp. She gestured him imperiously to a couch at one end of the room. He scampered off and sank into it, grinning hugely.

Heavy draperies of turquoise and aquamarine hung from the walls, with no windows in sight. Indirect lighting filtered out of the joints where the walls joined the ceiling. This light was captured on photosensitive plates at planet level, piped down by wire to the Caverna Gigantea, and there released by rheostat to the various photoelectric cells hidden within the walls of the palace and the houses of the kingdom. Because the illumination came indirectly, it did not matter that it was actually transformed sunlight. The blue pigmentation of the Azurians was not adversely affected by indirect rays.

The scene in the crystal was very clear. Azura stood by it, peering down in fascination.

She saw the hooded figures—her own agents, wrapped in hoods and robes and masks to protect them from the sunlight—and a strange blond man and a teenage boy.

"What is this?" she asked aloud. "My guards? And who is that young man?"

It was at that moment that Willie froze the guards into time and roused Flash from his paralysis.

"Oh-ho!" cried Azura. "It's Flash Gordon. And here on Mongo again. How delightful."

Qilp giggled on the couch and bounced up and down gleefully.

Azura paid him no heed. Her mind was traveling swiftly into the past, and as she remembered she felt her heart beat violently in her breast.

The sight of Flash Gordon still brought her to a kind of trembling ecstasy. She had met him some years ago, when he had been on Mongo, fighting at the side of Prince Barin.

"I loved you, Flash Gordon, beloved enemy," she said softly. "I suppose I'll always love you and here you've come back to me!" She smiled broadly.

Yes. She had loved him and he had refused her. She had offered him everything. The Kingdom of Blue Magic. Her own self as his queen. All the riches in the palace. Everything he wanted, just to be her king.

He had refused her.

It was that silly Earth girl, Dale Arden, Azura knew.

But it did not matter what reason he had. The fact that he had refused her was what rankled in her heart. She had sworn vengeance.

But he had escaped in that tricky way of his on the eve of the night set aside for their glorious wedding.

He had left her, and she had been the laughingstock of the entire palace entourage—not that she had seen anyone laughing at her in her shame. But she had put them all to death anyway, because she knew they wanted to laugh.

And she had killed them the slow, painful way: producing a toxic gas in the air that paralyzed them, keeping them fully awake, conscious, and sensitive to every touch on their bodies. Then she had alternately frozen them in below-zero centigrade dry air and boiled them in above one-hundred centigrade steam, until they had expired many hours later.

No one would ever laugh at Queen Azura!

Now he had returned. Flash Gordon, her love, her hate.

She wheeled from the crystal. "Qilp! What are you dreaming for?"

"Your Majesty!" Qilp cried, bouncing to his feet and padding over to her with his shambling gait.

"Get on those nozzle controls, will you?"

"Yes, oh, Queen Azura," Qilp said, running across the room to a curtain. He ripped the drapes aside and revealed a console in the wall with many gauges and dials.

"The jets," Azura snapped, moving over to stand behind him. "Quickly!"

Qilp reached out.

Azura was at the crystal again. She saw Willie and Flash take the axes and throw them away. She saw her hooded guards spring to life again. She saw the ensuing fight, and then she cried over to Qilp: "Now! Turn on that paralysis mist!"

"Yes, oh, Queen Azura," Qilp said, giggling.

The gas formed in the mouth of the cave at which Flash Gordon and Worriless Willie were staring, and swept out along the ground over the rocks toward them.

With a faint smile, Queen Azura watched. She knew they would not guess what it was at first: a gas that would turn them both into unconscious automatons in a split second.

She laughed.

"Blue Magic!" she whispered gleefully, rubbing her hands together and staring at the crystal with relish.

She saw Flash freeze, and then the teenage boy. She turned and gazed at Qilp with a kind of mad gloating.

"They are ours, Qilp. Ours!"

Chapter 8

Dr. Zarkov was fuming. He was fuming and puffing and talking at the same time, which took a little doing. Mainly, he seemed to be cursing to himself under his breath.

"That darned kid," he muttered again, kicking at a stone on the trail ahead of him.

Dale laughed. "Well, it serves you right, Doc. You played tricks on us to get us out to your place. Just because Willie's played tricks on you is no reason to take it out on him."

Zarkov raised his fists into the air and waved them about for a moment. "Maybe you're right," he growled suddenly. "But this is taking me away from my experiments."

"Your experiments with Willie, I suppose you mean," Dale said thoughtfully.

"That's right. Without Willie, I could not do the experiments, anyway." He looked at Dale and laughed in his booming way. "This whole thing is just one big long experiment, isn't it?"

Dale nodded. "So you'd better relax and enjoy it."

Zarkov slapped his hands together and looked around. "Dale, we're not getting anywhere on this trail. I think Flash and Willie took the right one."

He peered at the rocky crags ahead of him.

"This stuff is apparently some schist formation without any kind of geologic interest; the other formation, where we first arrived on Mongo, was much more exciting."

"The oceanite?"

"Right."

"What is oceanite, anyway?"

"It's a kind of blue igneous rock," Zarkov said. His eyes

lighted up. "Hey!" he boomed. "That's what I was trying to remember. It's the rock formation of the Caverna Gigantea."

"What's that?" Dale asked.

"The Kingdom of Blue Magic."

Dale's eyes opened wide. "You mean Queen Azura's lair?"

"I don't know if it's a lair or not," Zarkov said, smiling, "but it's Queen Azura's land, all right."

"She always had her eye on Flash," Dale said darkly.

"Yeah." Zarkov grinned. "You two never did seem to hit it off, did you?"

"She always wanted to claw my eyes out."

"And you? What did you want to do to her?" asked Zarkov.

"No comment."

Zarkov shook his head. "Dale, I vote we go back and meet Flash and Willie. Maybe the four of us can find our way out together. Now that we know where we are—"

"What was that?" Dale asked, turning her head to one side and listening.

"What?" Then he heard the distant sound of garbled cries.

"It's Flash and Willie!" snapped Zarkov, grabbing Dale's arm. "Come on. They're in some kind of trouble."

The two of them raced back along the trail they had taken. The pathway twisted down the side of the sliding schist formation, switchback after switchback. Dale had to slow down at every turn, or stumble over into the rocks that bordered the narrow trail.

Zarkov kept fuming and cursing the dust that rose from their boots.

The trail straightened out and soon they came to the spot where they had separated from Flash and Willie.

"Hold it," Zarkov called.

Dale stopped.

"Listen."

There was no sound at all.

Zarkov growled, "I don't hear a thing. What happened to Flash and Willie?"

Dale shook her head. She was worried. "We'd better hurry, Doc. Maybe they were outnumbered."

"I don't have a weapon of any kind," Zarkov said sourly. "And neither does Flash."

"It can't be helped. Come on."

"Darn that Willie," cried Zarkov. "I'd like to—"

Dale started to run along the trail that led into the bluish rock formation.

Zarkov stared after her, and then began to follow.

The trail was steep, but they soon found themselves at the top of the rise, staring down onto the cliff face at the point where Flash and Willie had been attacked by the hooded figures.

The summit of the mountain spine was deserted.

"Hey, Doc!" said Dale, kneeling on the ground and pointing into the dust. "Look at that."

Zarkov leaned over her shoulder. "What? I don't see anything."

"The print. It's Flash's bootprint."

"How do you know?"

"I bought them for him, silly. You see the circle and the square? That's a special brand Flash likes."

Zarkov rose and peered off into the distance across the vast wilderness that spread out from the foot of the cliff. "Well, if he's gone on from here, I don't know where he is at all."

Dale rubbed her chin thoughtfully. She peered around at the rocks and the trail. "Doc," she said slowly, "if anybody wanted to ambush us, this is the place they would hide, isn't it?"

Zarkov glanced about. "Yeah, I suppose so."

"Then maybe someone did ambush Flash and Willie."

"There's no doubt about it," Zarkov said worriedly. "But then where did the ambushers take them? The trail seems to end here."

Dale stared at the rocks. Suddenly, she moved her head and waved her hand at Zarkov.

"Doc! Look over there!"

She had seen the mouth of the cave. Zarkov came over and stood beside her, and he, too, saw the entranceway past the rocks.

"I'll be darned," Zarkov said. "It's a cave." His face paled. "Dale!" He grabbed her arm. "Look, we've got to get out of here right now!"

"What is it, Doc?" Dale asked in surprise. "I want to take a look at that cave. Flash may be in there, along with Willie."

"I know they're in there," Zarkov said in a whisper. He was pulling Dale along with him, retreating down the trail onto the other side of the mountain spine.

"But the cave—" Then Dale understood. "The cave leads to the Kingdom of Blue Magic."

"Exactly," whispered Zarkov. They were running now, down the mountainside. "We've got to get out of here, or that hussy will be sending out her hooded agents to grab us, too."

"But Doc we've got to help Flash. We're pretty sure he was fighting with some of Queen Azura's guards. And we've got to get to him."

"No way," snapped Zarkov. "We'll need a lot of help if we mean to force our way into the Caverna Gigantea—you know that. I'd say we've got to make it out of here to Arboria and get Prince Barin to help us mount an assault on the cave."

"Doc, that's a long way from here. How are we going to be able to help Flash now?"

Zarkov stopped running and sank down on a rock to rest. Dale stood beside him.

"We're exactly two days from Arboria, if that's the entrance to the Kingdom of Blue Magic," said Zarkov. "I remember that from one of Prince Barin's maps. And it's a long, hard walk."

"But what about Flash and Willie? They're probably in great trouble. Are we just going to leave them there?"

"What else can you suggest?" Zarkov asked stubbornly. "If we blunder in there, they'll simply capture us too."

"I suppose so," Dale agreed reluctantly. "I just hope we don't get to Prince Barin too late to do Flash and Willie any good."

"I agree," Zarkov said grumpily. "But I can't think of any other way to help them now."

"Nor I," Dale said dismally.

With Zarkov leading the way during the light of day, the two of them set off in a northwesterly direction from the site of the cave.

By nightfall, they had traversed quite a few Mongo miles, but still had not caught sight of any habitation.

"Of course," Zarkov said, "it's all desert here. This is the Great Mongo Desert's western border. We're lucky it isn't the eastern or southern border. The sun is fierce there, with no water anywhere."

"Is there water here?" Dale asked wearily. "I'm thirsty."

Zarkov burst out laughing. "Don't you hear the sound of a running brook, Dale?"

Dale listened. Her face broke into a happy smile. "Yes! Oh, Doc, you've been trying to fool me."

"I heard the sound a few moments ago. We'll rest up there, Dale, and go on in the morning."

"I wish I'd brought something to munch on," Dale said ruefully.

"Well, you never knew you were coming this far," Zarkov said with a frown. "Drat that Willie, anyway."

They came over the brow of the hill and there before them was an oasis of palm trees and green grass, still and quiet in the starlit night. The seventh moon of Mongo had not yet risen, but the stars were brilliantly reflected in the silvery water of the oasis.

The two of them moved over toward the water and drank slowly.

Dale lay down, looking up at the stars.

Zarkov muttered to himself.

"What is it, Doc?"

"I'm making calculations, that's all."

"Calculations?"

"Navigational calculations," he explained. "It's a lot more accurate steering by the stars, you know. In the morning, we'll go out in that direction," he said pointing, "and continue across the plains. We'll be heading directly for the woods of Arboria."

"At least it'll be cooler walking in the shade of the trees," said Dale.

"We'll get up early and walk before the sun gets high in the sky," Zarkov said, lying down beside the oasis. "Now get some sleep. I'll wake you before dawn."

Zarkov roused Dale while the moon was still in the sky, and they rose and started across the sandy expanse of desert. In a few minutes, they were walking through a fairly green plain that seemed a welcome relief from the sandy desert over which they had walked the afternoon before.

"What do you think of the Witch Queen, Doc?" Dale asked.

Zarkov grinned. "I think she's a very beautiful demon lady."

"Men!" snapped Dale. "Always thinking about looks!"

"Don't you?" Zarkov asked teasingly.

"I think of her as an evil woman," snapped Dale.

"Sure. An evil woman with Flash Gordon in her arms."

Dale flushed. "Stop it, Doc. It's not funny."

"Of course it isn't funny. You asked me what I thought of Queen Azura. She's beautiful—but she is a menace."

"And dangerous," said Dale.

"And dangerous. Now don't worry. We'll get to Arboria and Prince Barin will help us rescue Flash."

"You don't have much confidence in Flash's ability to get out of the Witch Kingdom, do you?"

Zarkov thought about that. "Queen Azura has a way with her, Dale. Don't forget she's got the best scientists on Mongo working for her. I think they've come up with every drug imaginable. And I think they can do almost anything scientifically. That's why she's so dangerous—and why we have to stop her. I'm surprised that the Free Council of Mongo, under Prince Barin, hasn't blasted her and that rough bunch of Azurians out of Inner Mongo yet."

"Maybe they haven't been able to," Dale suggested.

"Since Ming the Merciless was killed, there hasn't been any real need for fighting," Zarkov said. "The last interplanetary missive I received from Prince Barin said that Mongo had embarked on the most successful and prosperous era in the history of the planet."

"We're not even sure Flash has been taken to Azuria," Dale said apprehensively.

"We heard that shouting and crying," prompted Zarkov.

Dale nodded. "And we couldn't find him."

"The odds are he's been taken there along with Willie." Zarkov shook his head.

"Doc," Dale said uneasily after a moment.

Zarkov frowned. "What's the matter?"

She came up close to him and began to whisper. "I've got a funny feeling we're being followed."

"Who could it be?" scoffed Zarkov. "We're in the middle of the Great Mongo Desert!"

"I still have the feeling someone is watching us, or perhaps following us."

Zarkov glanced at the sky. He saw a large bird circling about in the distance, above the oasis they had just left. He turned to Dale. "There's a bird there. Is that what you're spooked by?"

Dale glanced into the sky, which was now growing more and more orange as the sun moved up toward the horizon.

"No," she said, shivering slightly. "I do feel it, Doc."

Zarkov slowed down. "I'll grant there is a kind of sense of a presence out there in back of us." He straightened. "But if there was someone there, why didn't they attack us in our sleep? It doesn't make sense that they would simply wait and follow us in the daylight."

"No," Dale agreed slowly.

They walked along in silence while the sky grew much lighter all around them.

"Doc!" screamed Dale, clutching Zarkov's arm.

Zarkov turned in shock and then stared past Dale's shoulder.

The two of them looked wide-eyed at the sky, where an enormous, man-sized bird was slowly swooping down toward them—a bird with an enormous wingspan and talons that resembled human hands with claws on the ends of its fingers.

Then, as they stared in anguish at the sky, another of the giant birds swooped in from another direction.

"Dale! Run! Run for your life!" screamed Zarkov, beginning to bolt as fast as he could for a clump of rocks nearby.

Dale panted after him.

Then, as they approached the rocks, with the big birds moving steadily nearer them, they were disheartened to see something rise in front of them.

Two more birds, bigger than those behind them, were standing on the rocks, looking at them. Six feet high from their heads to their talons, their wingspans at least sixteen feet fully open, they had enormous beaks and what appeared to be bald heads.

"Their faces," whispered Dale. "They're—they're—human beings!"

"Bird beings," Zarkov whispered back. "Not human beings."

The birdmen folded their wings, crossed their taloned arms over their chests, and waited. Dale saw their strange covered-over eyes, resembling racing goggles, through which the birdmen seemed to be studying them.

"What do they want?" Dale asked in a croaking voice.

Zarkov spoke, his voice shaking just a bit: "Us."

Chapter 9

Flash Gordon was conscious once again, but he could not move. He had been standing up when he had lost consciousness in the rocky pass outside the mouth of the cave to the Kingdom of Blue Magic.

Now he lay flat, placed on a vehicle of some kind, and he found himself stripped to the waist. He saw a great deal of activity going on around him. His young companion, Worriless Willie, also lay on the same vehicle, which was a large, open-bed carrier.

Hooded figures scurried about near him, and then, quite suddenly, the vehicle started to move. It rose into the air, turned once, descended, and entered the mouth of the cave.

Flash knew that he and Willie had been paralyzed by a formulation of nerve gas. The gas was the fog they had seen roll out of the mouth of the cave. He had been too stupid to move quickly enough to get Willie away from the dangerous vapor.

Trust Queen Azura to develop and use nerve gas, Flash thought. It was just possible that she had seen him and Willie in that crystal ball of hers. Magic! It was simply a matter of scientific vidscreen surveillance.

The vehicle they were lying on floated through the luminescent terrain of the enormous cave called the Caverna Gigantea by Mongo scientists. Flash remembered that within the core of the planet a gravity sled had been developed by Azurian technicians which had become their means of propulsion through the caverns of the underground kingdom.

The enormous grottoes that opened out above him were beautiful. Indirect lighting—stored sun's rays transmitted from the outside world into small storage cells—

formed weird shadows on the green-and-orange ceilings of the caverns through which they passed.

It was extremely quiet in the inner core of Mongo. Pools of water with scarcely a ripple on the surface lay on both sides of the cavernway through which they floated. Small eyeless fish shot through the waters. Flash did not know the names of any of them; undoubtedly Doc Zarkov would!

Amphibians from an earlier era of life stalked about on the distant rock shelves, their oversized eyes gleaming in the ill-lighted environment as they peered out at the human beings invading their private realm.

The gravity sled swooped past an enormous waterfall, over which plunged sparkling torrents of clear water for the people in the Kingdom of Blue Magic. A group of engineers in the traditional skintight leotards of indigo blue, worn by all of Azuria's people in the underground kingdom, paused in their work to eye the gravity sled bearing Flash and Willie.

Flash remembered the wealth of minerals embedded in the core of the planet that surrounded the Caverna Gigantea. It was a vanity of Queen Azura's to own it all, to dress herself in sparkling gems and to flaunt her riches to all strangers, to lord her wealth before all the peoples of Mongo.

The gravity sled took a turn and swooped downward swiftly, passing through several thousand feet of elevation in a few moments. On the lower levels of Azuria, the caverns widened out and led into a big valley. At the end of the valley, dappled with tiny pools of water and gardens of vegetation like algae and seaweed that did not need sunlight, Flash saw the jeweled spires of the city of Azuria itself, and, dominating the city, the spiraling tower of Azura's palace.

The sled zoomed over the valley and into the confines of the city. Sounds of bustling activity surrounded him, but Flash could not see below the sled.

They entered the palace through an oval slot that opened in a wall and immediately the gravity sled settled to the stone floor. The hooded drivers of the vehicle removed their cloaks and hoods and stretched their arms in the freedom of their iridescent indigo leotards.

A shaft of air enveloped the vehicle, its drivers, and its passengers, and they all rose steadily into the heights of the queen's tower.

Then, quite suddenly, they were settling down in a spacious, well-ventilated chamber illuminated by indirect reenergized sunlight. The chamber seemed to be a large group of rooms that had been made into a separate apartment, set aside from the rest of the palace.

Flash guessed that it must be Queen Azura's personal quarters.

At the end of the large area, a winding stairway led into an upper region where Flash saw several doors opening off a corridor. Heavy drapes hung from the walls; there were no windows.

Couches and tables and desks of various design stood about in the spacious area and the stone floor was covered with a richly brocaded carpet of a peculiarly exotic Mongo design.

The drivers turned to inspect Flash and Willie, and then moved quickly away from the gravity sled and vanished through an oval slot in the wall that closed once it had received them.

A brooding silence hung over the large spacious chambers. Flash saw no one at all about. Along one wall, he made out a series of small cupboards like wooden coffins raised on end. There were five of them; all were empty.

Flash closed his eyes and lost all sense of time. It seemed many hours that he lay there, waiting. Or it might have been only a few minutes.

Suddenly, a door at the far end of the chamber opened and a grotesque, capering figure four feet high entered, laughing and gesturing to someone behind him.

And then Flash saw Queen Azura.

Stately, commanding, smiling, and as evil as any one person could be, she entered the chamber behind the gibbering dwarf with a sweeping, queenly gait in total contrast to her jester's mien.

The monster jumped up and down, staring at Flash and Willie supine on the gravity sled, making faces, and laughing harshly. Queen Azura soon stood beside him, her eyes glittering with excitement.

She was as beautiful as she had been the first time he saw her, Flash realized. If anything, she was more beautiful. In this land where aging was controlled by scientific means, and health was a simple matter of a pill a day, beauty was the only possible condition of the human body.

Except for the dwarf. Flash wondered who he was.

"At last," Queen Azura said, sighing, leaning down over Flash and looking into his eyes. "We meet again, my friend," she said with an almost hissing sound to her voice. "I know you can see me. I want you to realize that you are totally in my control now, Flash Gordon. You've blundered badly, allowing yourself to be taken into the Land of Blue Magic."

Flash tried to open his mouth to speak the angry retort his mind willed him to, but he could not. He lay there, unable to move a muscle.

"Yes, my love. It was a nerve gas, called paralysis NG, projected from nozzles hidden in the face of the cliff. The vapor paralyzed you and left you prey to my guards of the upper reaches." She laughed. "Oh, it is worth all the jewels in my kingdom to see you like this, powerless and unable to resist—so handsome, so muscular, so beautiful to behold."

She leaned over him, lifting her trailing hand to touch his lips with her finger.

"How I recall the last time we met, when you rejected me, Flash Gordon." Azura's eyes turned dark with anger. "Rejected me!"

There was silence.

The dwarf jumped up and down and giggled. Queen Azura turned quickly, flinging her hand across his mouth and sending him sprawling end over end against the hard wall.

"Hey!" he cried. He staggered to his feet, touching his face which was bright red where she had hit him. "You shouldn't do that to me, Your Highness."

"I do what I want with my subjects," hissed Queen Azura. "You're lucky I didn't dip you in the acid pot, Qilp. Nobody mocks me."

"I did not mock, oh, Queen Azura!" Qilp whimpered. "After all, I am your trusted minister of intelligence. I simply enjoy the giant Earthling's helplessness."

Queen Azura turned from Qilp, her eyes once again moving over Flash's body. She was a beautiful woman, Flash thought. But evil and dangerous.

"Well, we must bring you out of your stupor, lovely Flash," Queen Azura murmured, again moving her hand to Flash's face and touching his cheek. "Then we shall see what happens to the brave Earth visitor."

She turned and clapped her hands loudly.

An oval aperture in the wall opened and a group of four bespectacled individuals came into the room. They stood around the gravity sled without further orders.

"Bring the big one to consciousness," snapped Azura.

"What about the small one, oh, Queen Azura?" asked one of the men.

"Put him in one of the suspension vaults, for the time being," the queen said after a moment's thought. She gestured vaguely toward the wall.

"Yes, Your Majesty," said another of the workers.

They approached the gravity sled. One of them peered through the thick lenses at Flash's face. He reached into his skintight leotard and removed a small box. It was full of capsules. He lifted one and brought it close to Flash's face.

"That'll be enough, Dr. Kluf," said Queen Azura. "Take care of the youth and leave me."

Dr. Kluf waved his hands at the others and they lifted Willie from the sled and carried him on his back over to one of the boxes lining the wall. Carefully, they turned him upright, and then placed him in the box. He stood there serenely, staring out into the chamber.

"Don't wake him," Azura snapped thinly.

"Yes, oh, Queen Azura," Dr. Kluf said, bowing, his eyes narrowed behind the lenses of his glasses.

What kind of eyes, Flash wondered, must these people need to see in this half-dark kingdom?

Azura clapped her hands and stamped her foot. "Out," she said.

"Me too?" Qilp asked with a leer.

"No," Azura said slowly. "You stay; I may need your help."

The two of them stared at Flash on the gravity sled.

"He should be coming around now," Queen Azura mused lazily. "Maybe this will speed up matters."

She leaned down over Flash and touched his lips with hers.

Qilp giggled.

Quickly, Flash grasped her wrist and held her tightly, so she could not move.

"Let me go," gasped Azura.

"You want to play games with me?" Flash asked roughly. "Then let's play."

Azura's face turned red. "Flash, I've been good to you. I gave you the antidote to the nerve gas. Now you be good to me."

Flash sat up slowly on the seat of the gravity sled and held her tightly against him.

"Don't joke with me. You haven't done a thing for me. You're still holding me captive." Flash smiled at her briefly. "Or possibly, I'm holding you captive."

Azura's face stiffened. "You're hurting me, Flash. I'll remember that when—" Azura fell silent.

"When what?"

She shook her head.

"All right," Flash said, shaking Azura's wrists and giving her a twist. "Give the antidote to Willie."

Azura's face was blank. "Who's Willie?"

Flash nodded his head toward the suspension vault where Willie had been placed.

"In that coffin you've got against the wall."

"Oh. You mean the silly little boy."

"Give him the antidote," Flash snapped. "And be quick about it."

"Is he your son, Flash?" Azura asked slyly.

"He's a good friend," said Flash.

"You've always played it so heavy with me, Flash. We're here together. What's wrong with relaxing a little? We can have a good time before I let you go."

Flash stared. "I don't believe you will let me go, Azura."

Her face twisted. "You aren't doing yourself any good grabbing hold of me like that," Azura said.

"I'll let you go if you tell that dwarf of yours to bring Willie out of his paralysis."

"I'm no dwarf," Qilp yelled indignantly.

"He can't do it, anyway," Azura assured Flash. "Only I can, or my scientists."

"Then do it."

"How can I act when you've got hold of my hands?" Azura pleaded.

"Tell me what to do," Flash ordered her. "I'll do it."

Azura's eyes narrowed. "There's a locket in the clasp of my cape," she told him.

Flash looked down at the clasp that held Azura's cape together in front of her throat. He saw a small jeweled locket.

"Open it," Azura commanded.

"If you're tricking me, Azura," Flash began threateningly.

"I swear," she said softly.

Flash opened the locket. There was a small capsule inside.

"Break the capsule," said Azura.

Flash glanced over Azura's shoulder at Qilp. The dwarf stared at him with no expression in his eyes at all.

With sudden resolution, Flash crushed the capsule.

Instantly, he felt a languor overtake his entire body. He smiled at Azura and let her go.

She rose and straightened her sheath dress, watching him carefully.

Flash leaned back and looked up at her. For some reason he was suddenly afraid, more terribly afraid than he had ever been in his life before.

"What is it, Flash?" asked Azura with veiled interest. "You look different."

"Yes, Earthman," Qilp said grinning evilly. "What is it?"

Flash shook his head. "Nothing." He closed his eyes and drew in a deep breath to steady himself. He could feel his flesh crawling, almost with terror.

Azura stood over him, reaching out her hand to him. "All right, Flash. Was I lying to you?"

Instinctively Flash recoiled from the touch of her hand. He drew back away from her, his whole body quivering with an atavistic fear he could not isolate.

"Go away!" he cried. He was astonished to hear his voice high and reedy and bordering on hysteria.

Azura threw back her head and laughed throatily.

Flash could feel cold perspiration on his forehead. "What are you laughing at?"

"It's a new preparation we've developed here in the Kingdom of Blue Magic," she said, her voice bubbling with mirth. "It makes cowards of the bravest of men."

"C-c-cowards," Flash stuttered, unable to say the word correctly. "I'm no coward!"

"Perhaps you weren't, Flash, but you are now."

Qilp giggled.

Flash frowned. He understood. "You tricked me. You made me break a capsule of this new formulation invented by your evil scientists."

"Exactly," Queen Azura crowed.

"But when I broke the capsule, why weren't you affected by it?"

"I stayed far enough away," said Azura. "It is called pacifist mist, Flash Gordon, but we also serve it in the food of those we wish to keep subdued."

"And if I refuse to eat?" Flash demanded.

"You starve to death, Earthman!" yelped Qilp.

Flash frowned. He was regaining some of his old courage. "But I won't let it work. I've got a stronger will than most people. I can think away fear."

Azura turned quickly to Qilp. "Run!" she ordered him. "Get your cousin here. I don't think that stuff is working."

Qilp bolted headlong across the chamber to the door and slammed it behind him.

"So," said Flash, jumping down off the gravity sled and advancing on Azura. "It's not working. It can make the average man a coward, but not Flash Gordon."

Azura backed away, her eyes showing momentary terror. "I think you may be the exception," she murmured and quickly touched her belt.

Flash saw the quick movement of her hand.

"What are you doing?"

But she had out another locket, and the fumes of the second capsule had risen to his nostrils before he could draw back.

The greatest terror gripped him. In the air around him suddenly, he could see the shapes of hideous monsters—things conjured from the imagination of a madman.

There were misshapen animals with pointed teeth, dripping blood. There were emaciated, wrinkled, hideous old crones, lifting talons to rake his flesh. A corpse of moldering putrescence floated toward him, screaming hysterically and reaching out to touch him with slimy fingers.

"Stop! Stop!" screamed Flash.

He fell back and crawled away from the phantoms in the air about him. Soon his shoulders touched the wall and he could go no further.

"Get them off me," he pleaded with Azura.

The queen laughed.

"I'm afraid. I'm afraid."

Through the haze of terror, he saw her look down at him.

"Silly man," she snarled. "Silly, foolish man. You could have been my king, but you chose instead to reject me. To fight me. You'll find out what it is to make an enemy of Queen Azura."

"No, no," Flash howled, pushing himself back against the wall. "Go away."

Azura laughed again, an evil, sinister laugh that made Flash's body quake with fear.

Chapter 10

Queen Azura was elated. Here, within her power through a combination of paralysis NG and pacifist mist, was the catalyst she needed for her final act.

She had been silly to be so worried about how to achieve her ends. Didn't something always happen at the last minute to put the whole scheme into focus?

Phase one of her plan had long been in the works, including the development of weaponry and military machinery—"hardware" as her minister of war called it—and also including a great deal of mass propaganda administered to her people through the controlled media under the administration of her ministry of communications.

And phase two was also very much in the works, although it was so deeply secret and so very much controlled by total security that no one in the realm really knew the truth about it. No one but Qilp. Of course, there were rumors, and the rumors kept bringing up the dreaded name of Ming the Merciless, although he had been dead for six years.

Queen Azura smiled at the thought of phase two.

And now, suddenly, here was phase three, ready to go. The sudden and unexpected arrival of Flash Gordon on the planet Mongo, and the almost unbelievable good fortune of having him drop into her hands, had caused her to think seriously of implementing phase three immediately.

And phase three would bring on phase four—all-out war.

Thoughts of phase two were a bit unnerving to Azura, but she knew she must face all the rather unpleasant possibilities involved in working with the principal factor of that action. Qilp would be back soon. She erased all thought of *that* from her mind.

Yes, Queen Azura was elated.

And she was also amused.

Paralysis NG, the nerve gas her experts in the council of scientific advisors had devised for her, was one thing, but this new formulation—pacifist mist—was something else again.

Originally, as part of her overall plan to dominate the planet of Mongo both politically and scientifically, she had moved her entire ministry of science into military experiments. The genius and ingenuity of the Azurian scientists had, however, come up with more and more types of vapors and formulations that had nothing to do with military aggression.

Pacifist mist was a strange offshoot from the labs that Azura had never tried to use before. Now, as she studied Flash Gordon cowering in the corner of her chamber, she realized that some of these military developments could be used for her own personal pleasure as well as for intraplanetary conquest.

Naturally, none of this would ever interfere with her ultimate goal—to become the Witch Queen of Mongo.

Meanwhile, she could afford to indulge herself with Flash Gordon, to whom she had once made a long-standing promise: to make him pay for spurning her advances years before when he had first landed on Mongo.

She knew his strength and his will and his pride. And now she had bested him by the very simple means of forcing pacifist mist on him. He had turned into a man without courage, a mouse, a cipher motivated totally by fear and terror.

Pacifist mist alone could make the average man into a cowering wretch, just as her lab technicians had promised. Yet it had not been powerful enough to defeat Flash Gordon completely. Her scientists had developed another vapor, pacifist mist plus, to be used in conjunction with pacifist mist if it proved not effective enough.

Plus was a vapor that accentuated the original fear inspired by pacifist mist by causing hallucinations in the mind, hallucinations based on fear and horror.

In effect, although pacifist mist had turned Flash Gordon momentarily into a coward, he had begun to fight off its effects by his own strong willpower and self-confidence.

But the fear vapor from pacifist mist plus had taken

hold of his mind and made him see nonexistent demons and monsters, at the same time turning him into a fearful, terror-stricken, demon-ridden human being.

Queen Azura laughed again.

"Well, Flash Gordon," she said triumphantly, standing over him, hands on hips, "I hardly recognize the proud, domineering man I once knew. What has happened to you?"

"Let me alone," muttered Flash, his face pale, his eyes sunken into his head. "Please."

"No," Azura responded with a smile. "I can't let you alone, Flash. You're going to help me."

"Go away," whispered Flash, turning his head to the wall.

Azura's face turned furious. "You sniveling coward, don't try to avoid me." She leaned over him and grabbed his shoulder, pulling him toward her. "Now get up."

"No, no," Flash said, moaning.

"Get up or I'll hit you," snapped Azura, and drew back one hand to slap his face.

Flash's eyes widened and his mouth trembled. He quickly scrambled to all fours, and then stood up beside her, towering over her, but trembling and pale.

"Don't hit me, Queen Azura, don't hit me."

Queen Azura smiled her satisfaction. "Enough of these quivering pleas, Flash."

She took his hand.

He cowered over her, and then as she smiled at him he allowed himself to be led by her across the chamber toward a trestle table that sat at the far end of the apartment. There were pencils and pens on the desk, an inkwell, and some piles of paper.

"Please, Queen Azura," whined Flash as she pulled him along after her, "don't hurt me."

"I won't do anything bad to you, if you do as I say," she assured him with a smile.

"Thank you, Queen Azura. Thank you."

"Sit down, please," she said firmly. Flash looked up at her pleadingly, his eyes clouded and fearful.

"Where?" he asked.

She pointed to a chair at the trestle table. "There."

"What must I do?" he asked.

Azura walked around to the other side of the table and took up a sheet of paper. She reached out and lifted a pen out of a holder, dipped it into a well of ink, and handed the pen to Flash.

"Write," she commanded.

"Yes," said Flash. "What do you want me to write?"

Queen Azura looked at the ceiling a moment, composing her thoughts. "Write this: 'My Dear Prince Barin.' "

Flash glanced up with a smile. "I know Prince Barin. You want me to write a note to him?"

"Yes," said Azura.

Flash wrote on the paper, and then looked up with pleasurable anticipation. "Now what?"

She thought a moment. " 'I am once again on Mongo, and have been captured by Queen Azura.' "

Flash's hand trembled.

"Well?" snapped Azura. "Write!"

"But—" Flash shrugged and wrote.

"Now," said Azura. "Write this. 'With me is a visitor from Earth, a young boy. The two of us have been sentenced to death.' "

Flash's face tightened. His eyes were woeful. Tears came into them. "Queen Azura, would you kill me and Willie? Would you?"

"Oh, stop sniveling and write," demanded Azura. "You want me to box your ears?"

Flash trembled and wrote.

She frowned. "Now write: 'You and you alone can save us from a terrible death by surrendering yourself to Queen Azura of Azuria, the Kingdom of Blue Magic.' "

Flash's face was covered with perspiration. "But Queen Azura, Prince Barin will never come. He knows you'll kill him if he does."

"He'll come," snapped Azura. "And then I'll have him where I want him. What does it matter to you, Flash? You'll be safe. You and that teenage boy. You'll be safe, no matter what; it's Prince Barin I want now."

"I thought you wanted me," Flash said slowly. He played with the pen and ink.

"Who'd want a trembling coward?" Queen Azura asked tauntingly.

"Why do you want Prince Barin?"

Azura leaned over the table and grabbed Flash's hand. "Write what I said," she snapped. "No more questions."

Shaking, Flash wrote what she had told him to.

She took the sheet, read it, and nodded, satisfied. "Now write: 'As soon as you have appeared before Queen

Azura, Flash Gordon and the Earth boy will be released, but come alone.'"

Weeping, Flash wrote the rest of the letter.

Queen Azura picked it up, glanced at it, and made him sign it. "Good boy," she said. "Very good boy."

Flash smiled through his tears.

"And I'll have Prince Barin in chains. Without him, the entire Free Council of Mongo will disintegrate, and then Ming and I will rule Mongo!"

Azura backed away and stared at Flash Gordon, the triumph making her heart beat fast and the blood rush into her face. She had been indiscreet in mentioning phase two, and the man involved in phase two, but it did not matter now—now that she had the note that would act as the catalyst.

"Ming?" quivered Flash Gordon. "But Ming was killed in the war between Mingo and Arboria six years ago."

"Oh, yes," said Azura. "Ming the Merciless indeed was killed."

"He had no offspring," Flash said carefully.

"None for the planet of Mongo to know," Azura said complacently. She folded her arms across her breast and stared contemptuously at Flash Gordon.

"Ming's son is here?" Flash asked anxiously.

"Forget it," ordered Azura. "I'm tired of all these questions."

"What good will it do to destroy Prince Barin's Free Council of Mongo?"

"Power, Flash," cried Azura. "For centuries, my people have been relegated to the subterranean regions of the planet, spurned and alienated from the peoples above. Never have we been given a voice in ruling the planet of Mongo. We have always hidden here in the dark like outcasts of the lowest order.

"I have had enough of this kind of subservience. I want to live on this planet like all the other free peoples do, free to walk about and not skulk in the dark down here in this nether world."

Azura walked back and forth, and she could feel the rage well up in her.

"But why not cooperate with Prince Barin?" Flash asked. "He's a reasonable man. Be part of the Free Council, Queen Azura."

"Barin is a tyrant!" screamed Azura. "We have had

nothing but trouble with him and the council. We're going to destroy them all!"

"We?" Flash repeated. "You—and the son of Ming?"

Azura wheeled on him. "We," she said softly.

There was a rap on the far door. Queen Azura turned toward it and said crossly, "Who is it?"

"Qilp," cried the dwarf. "I've got him!"

Queen Azura only then remembered that she had sent Qilp out after his cousin. Confused, she turned to Flash and then made up her mind.

"Come in," she called out. As she turned back to Flash, she smiled faintly.

The door opened and Qilp came running in, his bald head gleaming in the faint light. Behind him there was a movement in the doorway and than a tall man, deep-chested and boasting a powerful physique, stepped into the queen's chambers.

Azura watched Flash's face.

Flash had turned his head to watch Qilp, and now his eyes fell on the strapping man who had followed Qilp in.

"It's unbelievable!" he gasped. His face went pale. "Ming!"

Azura nodded. She knew how closely Ming the Second resembled his late father in all aspects, except for his physique, which was superior to his father's. But the narrowed face, the Mandarin mustache, the dark liquid eyes, the thick black hair—he was Ming rejuvenated, and no mistake about it!

The Second was clad in a sleeveless leather tunic and trousers, with soft hide boots. He stood there a moment in the doorway studying Azura, and then his eyes moved to Flash Gordon.

The two men watched each other covertly for a moment. Azura was pleased to see Flash turn pale and look away after a moment's scrutiny.

"So this is the great Earth hero," Ming the Second said in a resonant, sneering voice that filled the queen's apartment.

Qilp giggled and ran behind Queen Azura.

"And we've got you right where we want you, haven't we?" Ming the Second continued, striding across to stand at the writing table opposite Flash.

"I knew your father," Flash said softly.

"That's where you and I differ," Ming the Second

snarled, his face darkening with rage. "I never even saw him."

"I—I didn't mean to offend you," quivered Flash.

Ming slammed a fist onto the trestle table, almost upsetting the inkstand.

"Then don't mention him. I hate him." Ming backed off and put his hands on his hips, surveying Flash carefully.

"No decent man hates his father," Flash said, his head up, his eyes for the moment defiant.

"Mine was a traitor—a traitor to me," cried Ming the Second. "Why shouldn't I hate him?"

"Why do you?" Flash asked calmly, trying to still the trembling in his arms and shoulders.

Ming paced restlessly around the trestle table as he spoke. He seemed unable to stand in one place for long, or to sit at all. He seemed the kind of man who always had to be on the move, always on the attack, always in the grip of his aggressions.

"He sired me by one of the slave ladies in the Kingdom of Blue Magic, and never took me to the palace of Mingo to rear me," complained Ming, his deep voice echoing in the queen's apartment. "I was brought up a captive here in this darkened subterranean kingdom—with that for a cousin!" Ming flung his hand contemptuously out toward Qilp.

Qilp capered and giggled and jumped up and down. He stuck out his tongue, and ducked behind Queen Azura. "Ming the Great, Ming the Great!" Qilp yelped in a parrotlike cackle.

Ming took a step toward the dwarf, his hand cocked menacingly.

Azura slapped at Ming's hand. "Watch your temper, Ming," she said softly. "Don't forget that I'm your queen and that you take orders from me."

Ming turned to stare blindly at her, rage contorting the muscles in his throat. Finally, he regained a semblance of control.

"Yes, Your Majesty," he said sarcastically. He turned on Flash. "The son of Ming, brought up far from the court where Ming the Merciless ruled. Brought up in exile, with this deformed monster as blood kin. Reared secretly, with only nurses and my slave mother in attendance. Bah! The son of an emperor—and growing up like any other child in a foreign land. Do you wonder why I hate my father?"

Flash shrugged. "He was still your father."

"Was," corrected Ming the Second. "Yes. And now I am as good as he ever was—yet I do not rule my kingdom, do I?"

"Whose fault is that?" asked Flash.

"It is not mine, Earthling. Not Ming's. It is the fault of this miserable Prince Barin, who has made subjects of all the peoples of Mongo. It is he who has usurped the country that was mine."

"Prince Barin has brought peace to Mongo," Flash said stolidly.

"Peace?" asked Ming. "What kind of peace is it to have all nations bow and scrape to Arboria and the weakling who rules it?" Ming whirled about and paced the length of the queen's chambers, glowering and silent.

"It will not be long," Azura said softly.

"No?" challenged Ming, turning on her and giving her a scathing look.

"I promise you," said Azura, her anger rising like a lump in her throat. "I promise you we will win."

Ming gestured with his hand and turned to Flash with a sardonic grin. "Women talk, men fight. All I've had since I've been a captive in this miserable kingdom is talk, talk, talk. And"—his eyes narrowed—"love and romance—the sick little things that delight women. Bah! Gordon, you're made of better stuff. You know why I'm wasting my time here, don't you? Because the time will soon come—"

"The time is now," interjected Azura.

Ming checked himself and turned slowly on her. There was a murderous look in his eyes. "Queen," he said, "I don't believe you, anymore than I've believed you for the past six years with your promises, promises, promises!"

Azura strode angrily to the trestle table and picked up the letter Flash had written.

"I've got Prince Barin on a hook, Ming. He must come here to free Flash Gordon. When he's here, we'll kill him."

Ming stared at her in disbelief. His lips moved soundlessly. Then he reached out and took the paper. He read it slowly, moving his lips as he read, and then let it flutter to the tabletop.

His face changed. The rage and hate left it, and a kind of sly excitement possessed it. He paced then, as he always did when excited, and he kept crashing one fist into the other palm as he raced about over the chamber's carpeted stone floor.

"Yes!" he said. "You're right. We'll get him here that way, and it'll be the end of him. The end."

Azura smiled and folded the paper carefully.

Ming wheeled suddenly and strode over to Flash where he sat at the table.

"And you," he yelled, pounding the table madly, "we'll kill you, too!"

"But," Flash whispered, "Queen Azura said when Prince Barin came, she'd let me go and let Willie go."

"Why should we let you go?" Ming asked in great astonishment.

"I want that letter," Flash said, rising and reaching for Azura's arm. "I must destroy it."

Ming smashed Flash's arm away from Azura. "Get your hands off her!"

Flash cowered, almost falling over backward.

"Don't hurt me, Ming!" he cried out. "I didn't do anything bad to you."

Ming stood back, gazing at Flash with disgust. "I heard you were a man, Gordon. I see a coward. Can't you fight?"

Azura touched Ming's arm. "He's under the influence of pacifist mist," she told him in a whisper. "I'm keeping him that way so he won't escape."

"He couldn't escape," sneered Ming. "As a matter of fact, I think you've all been lying about Flash Gordon. He hasn't any guts at all. He won't even fight. You've been joking."

Azura felt sudden anger. "You fool, he's only docile because of the drug."

Ming shook her off. "Come on, Gordon, let's have some fun. Man to man. A duel? How about a duel?"

Flash stood up and looked at Ming. "What kind?"

"To the death, Gordon!" Ming laughed loudly.

Azura strode forward, grabbing Ming's arm. "Stop it, you idiot!"

Ming threw her hand off his arm and turned to her, his face dark with rage. "Don't cross me."

Azura froze. She realized she was afraid of him, even though his interference might ruin everything.

An expression of contempt flitted across Ming the Second's features, and he turned from her. "Come on, Gordon. Let's fight."

"All right," Flash said, trying to quell his trembling.

Ming's eyes darkened in secret triumph.

Chapter 11

Ming was eager to fight. He had always prided himself on his excellent reflexes. Now the excitement of an encounter with the famous Flash Gordon—the man who had become a legendary character in Mongo's history in his own time—made Ming want to test himself against this giant-sized hero.

He studied his adversary for a brief moment, the curl of his lips giving vent to his inner contempt. Why, this so-called hero was nothing more than a sniveling coward. And even though Azura claimed it was all due to the pacifist mist, there must be a great deal of latent cowardice in a man who would become such an abject poltroon from a dosage of the drug.

The truth, Ming reasoned, probably lay somewhere in between. Quite possibly, the drug was having an effect on Flash Gordon, and quite possibly he had been built up to be more than he was because of the repetition of the legend.

Ming had no false modesty about his own prowess in battle. He was good. And he loved to feel the strength of his muscles in conflict against those of a contender. He loved to test his reflexes against those of any opponent.

"We'll fight!" he cried gleefully when Flash finally agreed. Ming spun on his heel and stalked across the floor to a large trophy case hanging on a wall of the queen's chambers.

"Ming!" Azura cried in dismay.

He ignored her. Reaching up, he opened the glass case and lifted down one of the two heavily decorated swords hanging in the case. He turned and laughed at Flash.

"Gordon," he said, "I'm ready when you are."

Flash's face paled. "I—I don't think I'd like to fight. I don't feel well."

"You feel as well as you're going to feel around here, Gordon," snapped Ming, advancing toward him with the sword extended. "Here, take it or I'll push the blade through your gizzard."

Flash rose unsteadily and reached out to take the sword.

Ming thrust it at him, watching his eyes. Flash took the sword by the hilt and held it in his hand, his eyes fearfully focused on Ming's face.

Laughing, Ming strode back to the trophy case and took out the second of the pair of beautifully jeweled dueling swords from a long-past historical era on Mongo.

He stood with the sword in position and studied Flash carefully. "So this is the legend," he muttered sardonically. "The fearless champion of the people, the indestructible enemy of the Emperor Ming, my father."

Flash wiped the perspiration from his forehead.

"Hah!" snapped Ming. "I believe I can do what all my father's armies could not. *En garde,* Gordon," he called.

"Ming!" cried Azura, running over and grabbing Ming's right arm. "Stop it. He is drugged, and we still need him."

Ming turned to the beautiful queen and arched a brow sarcastically. "Never fear, Azura. There will be life left in him when I have finished. Some life, that is." Ming threw back his head and roared with derision.

"No," Azura responded in annoyance. "Leave him alone."

"Come on, Gordon," snarled Ming, pushing Azura aside and moving toward Flash with his sword out in front of him. "You have been said to have crossed foils with a dozen men at once. Show me some of your prowess."

"There is no fight left in him," Azura warned him.

"Even a cowardly mouse will fight to escape."

With that, Ming lunged toward Flash, thrusting his sword toward the Earthman's naked chest.

"No—no!" screamed Flash. "Don't!" He staggered backward away from Ming's sword and cowered against one of the pillars that supported the ceiling of the queen's chambers.

Ming threw back his head and roared.

"I—I don't want to fight," whimpered Flash, standing behind the pillar and peering around it at Ming. "I don't want to die."

"Look at him," Ming growled happily. "The mighty

Flash Gordon. He whines like a woman, like the woman Azura."

"Ming, I'm warning you," snapped Azura, hovering in the shadows and frowning darkly.

"I wonder how he will sound when he's felt the sting of my sword?" cried Ming, and made a harsh feint at Flash with his sword.

Flash fell back into the shadows behind the pillar and Ming burst out laughing again.

"Ming," Azura said in a hushed voice, running up and standing beside him. "It is the drug, not your sword or your prowess, that makes Flash run."

Ming grabbed her shoulder and squeezed it tightly until she winced. "All the better, fair Azura. Then his torment is to your credit."

Azura threw off his hand and pulled away from him, giving him a bleak scowl as she kneaded her shoulder where he had touched her. "You've hurt me, you big lout."

Ming leaned down and stared into her face. "Does a small spot of an old affection spoil your pleasure, my beloved?"

"Pleasure?" Azura's eyes flashed.

"Your ancient love affair with the Earthman, dearest Azura," Ming said sardonically. "One would almost believe you still had a soft spot in your heart for him, even as he cowers in the shadows!"

Ming's voice dripped with contempt.

Azura straightened. "What's between Flash Gordon and me is none of your business at all, my love. If I hear one more word about it, I'll—"

"You'll what?" Ming turned to her.

Azura faced him, her lips flat and grim. "There is no pleasure for me in watching my noble emperor-to-be prove his clumsy stupid cowardice," she snapped. "Even in his terror, Flash Gordon is your match any day of the week."

Ming stared. It was obvious that Azura was not teasing him; she meant every word of it.

Ming's neck muscles tightened. His heart beat faster. He could feel his muscles knot up. The sword moved uneasily in his hand.

"Azura," he said in a low tone, "you always have the ability to stir me—one way or another. Now you stir me to rage and I'll have Gordon's blood for that."

"You fool," shouted Azura. "If you hurt him—"

Her fingernails ripped at his naked shoulder, and the pain shot through him. He saw red. Whipping around, he grasped her by the neck and threw her from him, so he could go after Flash.

Azura was cursing as she lay on the floor, her cape soiled and torn by the force of her fall.

"So!" yelled Ming, waving the sword and running toward the pillar where Flash skulked in the shadows. "My queen challenges me to test your valor, Flash Gordon. *En garde,* Earthman. *En garde!*"

He could see the form of Flash Gordon in the darkness behind the pillar and he lunged toward the muscular body, but even as he struck the portion of shadow where he thought Flash was he realized that the Earthman had tricked him. Staggering, Ming stopped his headlong lunge and turned around.

There he was, damn him, running up the stairs at the end of the queen's chamber—up to her bedroom!

"Try to run from me, will you?" bellowed Ming. He took out after Flash, waving his sword.

"Stop it, you two!" wailed Azura, on her feet now, and trying to restore order.

"Too late, my dearest one," shouted Ming, starting up the steps after Flash.

Flash turned and saw Ming pursuing him. With a frightened little cry, he gripped his own sword and waited for the big athletic fighter to come up the stairs two at a time, waving his weapon.

"Prepare to die, Earthling!" yelled Ming.

Instead of dying, Flash suddenly leaped up onto the marble banister of the winding stairs, and slid quickly down past Ming, who swung his sword ineffectually at him as he hurtled on past.

Ming waved the weapon above his head again. "You're an impudent wretch," he said softly, his face suddenly red with rage. "I'll get you. If that's the kind of cat-and-mouse game you want to play, I can play it too."

He ran down the steps after Flash, who had jumped to the stone floor, and was now running across it toward the draperies that concealed one wall near the stairs.

Azura was in a frenzy. "Stop it, stop it!" she screeched. "Qilp, will you stop them?"

Qilp, who had been watching the action from behind the protection of a large chair, giggled. "Not me."

Azura ran toward Ming, intercepting him as he went after Flash Gordon.

He looked down at her, standing defiantly in front of him. Something in her demeanor warned him and he paused, but his wariness of her did not prevent a sardonic smile from crossing his lips.

"Well, good Queen Azura," he grated out. "What is it this time?"

"You're making a silly ass out of yourself," Azura said angrily.

Ming felt the hackles on the back of his neck stiffen. "Nobody calls me a silly ass, my lovely queen, not even you!"

"I call a silly ass a silly ass," retorted Azura. "Now pack up that sword and get out of here. I've got work to do."

"So have I, woman," said Ming, reaching out to push her aside.

"Important work, you blundering idiot," cried Queen Azura. "I intend to bring Prince Barin here and conquer the planet of Mongo once and for all. Are you such a dolt that you can't see how?"

Ming stared past the beautiful woman's shoulders at Flash Gordon, standing there like some kind of drained puppet, and the rage and envy and hatred in him welled up and distorted his vision.

"Our of my way, you slattern!" he roared, and moved past her, shouldering her roughly aside.

She stared after him, her eyes black with hate.

"Ming—" She caught herself. "Oh, what's the use?" she asked herself, and shook her head briefly, before folding her arms across her breast and watching him.

He ran swiftly toward Flash Gordon, poised and ready to place the sword's point in the Earthman's heart. Flash did nothing to protect himself. In fact, he had dropped his sword to the floor and now stood there waiting for the attack with shaking knees.

"Touché!" shouted Ming, and thrust directly into Flash's heart.

But as he did so, Flash Gordon's heart was no longer there.

Ming stumbled forward and almost went down on all fours before he could bring himself upright and wheel to find out where Flash Gordon had gone.

"Damn you," he screamed.

Flash had grabbed onto the hanging drapery and was already climbing high above the surface of the floor, looking back over his shoulder in fright.

Ming ran over, waving his sword, and cursing because he could not reach the Earthman with it.

"Damn you, you circus clown!" yelled Ming. "Come on down and fight like a man."

Azura was shaking her head grimly. "Oh, bravo, Ming! Triple bravo! I am amused, but it is not Flash Gordon who plays the buffoon."

Ming ran to the drapery and tried to climb with one hand. He slipped and fell. His sword fell. He rose, picking up the sword, and gazed upward at Flash Gordon who clung in the middle of the drapery twenty feet above him, looking down like some kind of taunting rhesus monkey.

Ming gripped the sword, looked up at Flash, and said, "Try to make a fool out of me, will you?"

And Ming ran up the winding stairs which ended at the top of the drapes. Flash watched him fearfully. He looked down and saw the twenty-foot drop, and his face turned white. Then he looked at Ming quickly mounting the stairway, and his teeth began chattering.

"Try to run, will you!" Ming yelled, moving closer to Flash as he clung to the drape. "Cringing clown!"

Ming leaped three steps to the top and leaned out over the banister, slashing his sword at the drapery just above Flash's head.

"No!" shouted Azura from where she stood watching.

The drapes began to part where Ming's sharp sword had severed the material.

"You can't hide from me forever!" shouted Ming, cutting the drapes again.

The last thread that held them together parted, and Flash screamed.

"No! I'm going to fall!"

And no sooner had he said it than he did.

Ming watched the drapes and Flash Gordon slam down onto the stone floor of the queen's chambers. Ming felt his heart pound with exhilaration. He raced down the stairs, waving the sword in triumph.

There lay Flash Gordon unconscious on the stones, the cut drapes covering half his body.

Ming flew down the steps and paused over him, lifting his sword high.

"Now, you silly clown, here's an end to you."

Azura grabbed his arm again, pulling harder this time. "You fool! Put down that sword. You'll spoil all our plans for an empire in this insane envy of yours."

Ming shook his head. Maybe she was right. Maybe. . . . Flash Gordon looked so stupid, lying there on the floor that way. Ming straightened. Gordon was a clod. He started to laugh.

"When he's served our ends," Azura said in his ear, "then you'll have your turn with him—I promise that. But beware mighty Ming, I may not keep him drugged with pacifist mist then."

Ming threw his sword onto the floor, where it clattered loudly against the stones under the carpet.

"Never mind, lovely queen," Ming retorted in kind. "Drugs or no drugs, I'll finish him off. I owe it to myself, now. When he goes, it will prove that Ming is greater than he."

"Yes, Master Ming," Azura said softly.

He turned on her. Without warning, he reached out and took her wrists in his hands. Her wrists were cold. He drew her toward him, her body trembling as she strained against his grip.

"Don't give me orders," Ming said in a quiet but deadly voice. "Just don't give me orders."

She tore herself out of his grasp, rubbing her wrists angrily.

"Get out. Qilp and I will take care of Gordon." She turned and called out, "Qilp!"

The dwarf capered up.

"Ah, yes, Cousin," Ming snarled sourly. "I keep forgetting you are a power in this palace. Minister of intelligence, is it?" Ming laughed softly.

Qilp did not hear him at all. He was close to Queen Azura, and she was speaking softly in his ear.

Ming watched them as he slowly walked away. Qilp had been a good entrée for him into the palace. What power he had with the queen was only to the good. Once Ming did become emperor, then he wouldn't need Qilp anymore. Qilp. Or the ministers of science. Or Azura.

Or Azura. . . .

Meanwhile, it was good to have someone like Qilp close to the queen. After all, in a showdown, blood was always thicker than water.

Still, he liked Azura—when she obeyed him.

Chapter 12

Dr. Zarkov was not accustomed to the feeling of cold fear that he now experienced at the sight of the huge humanoid birds that had settled in a tight circle about the two of them.

"What'll we do, Doc?" Dale asked in a whisper, moving closer to him.

Zarkov glowered at the strange beasts. It was then that he straightened and squinted against the glare of the newly risen sun. Were his eyes playing tricks on him? Were these the killer birds he had taken them for? Or were they something quite different, something quite—?

"Dale," he murmured. "Don't you see? They're Hawkmen."

"Hawkmen?" she repeated, puzzled. Then her face broke into a smile. "But the Hawkmen were always friends of Prince Barin's, weren't they?"

"Indeed, yes!" cried Zarkov, his voice booming out. "All we have to do is tell them who we are."

"Wait," Dale said cautiously. "Are you sure you can convince them of our identity? No one knows we're even on the planet of Mongo yet."

"Except Queen Azura," Zarkov muttered darkly. "Well," he said, "there's nothing for it but to make ourselves known to these—uh—fine men." His voice trailed off.

"How?" Dale asked.

Zarkov fidgeted. Actually, the only way to do it was for Zarkov to walk up to the obvious leader of the Hawkmen and introduce himself. And yet as he stood there, staring about him at the menacing ring of winged men, he could not generate the same enthusiasm in himself that he projected in his voice.

Finally he pushed out his chest, extended his right hand in an open and friendly salute, and started across the sandy stretch between the poised birdmen and himself. "Friends!" he said loudly and hopefully.

As he approached, he could see that these men/birds were indeed Hawkmen, and not birds. Hawkmen on patrol wore skintight trunks with shoes of soft leather, and long shoulder-length gloves made of tightly woven chain mail ending in iron claws on the fingers. These talons served as weapons with which the Hawkmen fought.

On their heads, Zarkov saw the familiar shining helmets, with the extended wing insignia and the rank across the front. He saw that the man in charge was of captain's rank, the double-chevron insignia painted in the middle of the steel helmet.

The most curious physical feature of the Hawkmen was the large pair of wings extending from each scapula upward and downward. These wings were identical to a large bird's wings: the same muscle attachments, the same bone growth, and the same feathered integument.

Somewhere in Mongo's past, the mammal and the reptile had continued together in the same organism to pass into the mammal-bird phase—and the Hawkmen were the result.

However, the Hawkmen of Mongo did not possess the typical bird's superior vision. Because of that, Hawkmen patrols wore extremely thick antihelio tinted lenses that were corrected to bring the average individual's visual acuity to the equivalent of 20-05 or 20-04.

This made the Hawkmen, for their vision and for their maneuverability, the obvious national group to patrol the planet of Mongo for the Free Council.

"I'm Zarkov!" He halted ten feet from the captain of the Hawkmen.

The Hawkman smiled. He held his hands with the steel talons in front of him, waiting for any odd move from Zarkov.

"Indeed," the captain of the Hawkmen said.

"Dr. Zarkov," Zarkov repeated, frowning. "I've spent years on Mongo. I'm from Earth. Doesn't Prince Barin ever talk about Zarkov?"

The captain turned to the Hawkman nearest him, a sergeant. "Well?"

The sergeant stared at Zarkov. "I don't know, Captain Vogl," he told his commander.

Vogl stared at Zarkov. "Of course I've heard of Zarkov. He's a legend among our people. There are tomes about him in the Free Council of Mongo's libraries."

Zarkov turned to Dale. "You hear that, Dale? I'm in the libraries!" he boomed.

Vogl advanced. "But how am I to know you're really Zarkov, and not some imposter?"

"Don't I look like Zarkov?" Zarkov called out. "Don't I sound like Zarkov? There's only one Zarkov, dammit!"

Captain Vogl turned to his sergeant. "I would guess that he is who he says he is," he muttered.

The sergeant held up a hand. "I'll vidflash the Free Council for verification."

"And about time, too," Zarkov said moodily.

The sergeant drew a small black case out of his flying pack and twisted a lens on its front. "Stand right there, you who call yourself Dr. Zarkov. I'll send your image to FCM Identification Center."

Captain Vogl smiled sardonically. "Cheese, Dr. Zarkov. Cheese."

Zarkov smiled, lifted his head, and mugged slightly. "There. How's that?"

The sergeant flicked off the vidflash and raised it to his ear.

"What are you doing out in these forsaken spaces?" Zarkov asked Vogl conversationally.

"This is our patrol sector," Vogl explained, waving an arm about him. "All this area of the Great Mongo Desert."

"When did you pick up our track?" Zarkov wondered.

"Last night," Vogl said with a smile.

"But you didn't make yourself known—"

"We didn't want to," Vogl cut in. "We preferred to see what you were up to. When you began again to approach the disputed border of Arboria, we decided we must intercept you to find out your mission."

"Our mission is one of peace," Zarkov said.

"That remains to be seen," Vogl said, smiling.

"Flash Gordon was with us," Zarkov said. "He's been seized by Queen Azura's men."

For once, Vogl's calm face froze. "Flash Gordon?"

"You believe me?"

"Perhaps I do," Vogl said, looking at Zarkov intently through his enormous goggles. "We are checking out violations of the border attempted by Azura's troops."

"Ah-ha!" Zarkov cried out. "You hear that, Dale?"

Dale had approached and now stood at Zarkov's side. "Yes, Doc, you don't need to bellow."

"So there was a reason to seize Flash," Zarkov muttered. "And now that she's got him—"

The sergeant moved forward. "Confirmed," he said to Captain Vogl. "It's Dr. Zarkov."

"And about time you admitted it, too," Zarkov said testily. "Come on, come on. We've got to get to Arboria immediately. We must see Prince Barin."

Vogl held up a hand patiently. "Not so fast, Dr. Zarkov. We can't fly you out of here on our backs, you know."

"Too tough for you?" Zarkov wanted to know.

"It simply wouldn't be seemly," Vogl said evenly.

Zarkov let his hands rise and fall against his sides. "Then how?"

Vogl turned to the sergeant. "Radio back to Arboria for the heliocab, Sergeant, if you please."

"Right away, Captain."

Within minutes, a comfortable, four-seated, rocket-powered vehicle came into sight and zoomed to a quiet landing on the desert sand. It had a bubbletop of dark-blue glass which covered the entire passenger area.

"Beautiful job," Zarkov said, staring at the workmanship enviously. "Why the blue glass?"

"It serves a double purpose," Vogl explained as he gestured the driver to remain in the heliocab. "It keeps the sun's rays from burning the passengers, for one."

"I see," Zarkov said.

"That, however, is actually a secondary purpose. The primary purpose of the glass is to collect the rays of Mongo's sun."

Zarkov pouted. "You mean that's how the rockets are powered? By the sun's heat?"

"Yes," said Vogl. "A little something the scientists of the Free Council of Mongo have dreamed up."

"But there isn't enough energy from the sun to power the average rocket thrust," Zarkov muttered.

"True," Vogl agreed.

"Then what are you talking about?" Zarkov asked.

"Yes," Dale chimed in. "What are you talking about? I don't understand anything."

Zarkov turned to her. "Solar rays can be used to heat houses, you know, Dale. But there simply isn't any way to store enough solar energy to start up a rocket."

"Oh, I see," said Dale, not seeing.

Vogl gestured toward the heliocab. "The sun's heat is stored in the blue glass, and diverted into storage condensers. A simple-enough process."

"Yes, yes," Zarkov said impatiently. "But—"

"Once in the condensers, the energy is immediately put through a transformer to skim a little energy off the top."

"Go on," Zarkov said grudgingly.

"The extra heat is recoupled to new heat coming in from the blue-glass stores. That total portion is halved, with the first half going into the condensers, and the second half into the rocket mechanisms. As this type of regeneration is multiplied time and time again, the heat builds up a tremendous amount of excess, which, in turn, causes the rocket engines to start up. Excess heat from the operation of these engines goes back into the condensers and into storage to be reused in conjunction with the incoming sun's rays. It's a multiple regenerative multi-stage helio-powered rocket, according to our engineers," Vogl finished slowly.

Zarkov shook his head. "You sound like a scientist rather than a captain, Vogl."

"I started out to be a scientist," Vogl said carefully.

"Didn't work out?"

"I liked flying better," said Vogl. "It's an old family tradition." He moved his wings with a smile.

Zarkov nodded.

He and Dale stepped into the heliocab as the driver held up the bubbletop, and when they had settled into the remarkably cool double seats in the rear, the operator closed the bubbletop and climbed into the driver's seat.

Through the blue glass, Zarkov and Dale saw Captain Vogl waving to them and pointing northward, where the driver then aimed the heliocab and began his easy and even ascent into the Mongo sky.

"The thing drives without the least vibration," Zarkov said in awe. "They've certainly made great strides on Mongo since I was here."

Dale suppressed a smile. "Is that so strange, Doc?"

Zarkov frowned, turning to Dale. "You're joking with me," he boomed. "Stop that, Dale."

She laughed at his fierce expression.

He relaxed and leaned back.

Below them, they saw the vast expanses of the Great

Mongo Desert pass by as the heliocab rose and threaded its way through the thin air above.

A voice sounded inside the heliocab. "We're approaching the Great Northwest Sector," said Captain Vogl.

Zarkov glanced aside. Vogl was flying alongside the heliocab and was speaking into a small breastbone microphone around his neck. He pointed downward. Zarkov leaned over and looked at the desert below. From the sky, he saw the remarkable upthrusting of volcanic formations that dotted the landscape.

"It's also called the Lava Flats," Vogl remarked. "There's still volcanic activity at times here, although nothing has blown for some three years now."

Zarkov nodded. "It sounds like the skipper of an Earth jet from Metropolis West to Metropolis East announcing the sights," he told Dale with a grin.

Dale nodded. "It's beautiful in a crude kind of way," she said, pointing down at the volcanic formations.

"Now we're coming to the edge of the Great Mongo Jungle," said Vogl, pointing up ahead.

Zarkov saw the slight line of vegetation coming up on the horizon that up to that point had been all sand and lava. As they neared, the vegetation got greener and greener until they approached its edge, where the sunlight cast a thin black shadow of definition against the edge of the sand.

Then they were over a dense and tangled mass of vegetation, without a glimpse of earth or water beneath.

"The Great Mongo Jungle continues for some miles, and then we get into Arboria," said Vogl.

The jungle eventually petered out into a system of swampy, irregular canals and ponds that became one large lake, and then thinned into a stream.

The vegetation changed, and the dense jungle below vanished to be replaced by a forest of very large and sturdy coniferous trees.

"Arboria," Vogl said briefly.

They continued for some fifteen minutes, and then the craft began to lose altitude.

"We're beginning our approach to the city," Vogl explained.

"Arboria," Zarkov said to Dale. "I remember it well."

They descended until they were on the tops of the dense trees, with the bottom of the heliocab skimming the branches, and then suddenly there was an opening in the trees ahead. A kind of widened runway extended up through the forest, supported at a level by the trees on its borders.

The heliocab settled onto the runway with a soft snick of plyofoam and the heliocab was no longer airborne, but rolled along on conventional wheels toward Arboria.

Captain Vogl zoomed upward with his squad of Hawkmen, waving at Zarkov and Dale in the heliocab.

"We'll be going back now to our zone. Good luck, Dr. Zarkov, Miss Arden."

Zarkov and Dale nodded and waved in return.

The heliocab zoomed down the runway, which then converted into a regular roadway as it descended to the trunks of the trees. Then suddenly in the distance ahead they both saw the capital city of Arboria, a gleaming collection of towers and spires in the middle of the thick vegetation.

The heliocab slowed down; they maneuvered several intricate turns, and then they were going through a tunnel hollowed in an enormous tree from some earlier age. Finally, they were out on the palace grounds with the palace rising before them high in the trees.

The heliocab pulled up in a slot that had been made for it in the palace parking lot, and the driver turned.

"We're at the palace, Dr. Zarkov," he said respectfully.

"Thanks," said Zarkov. "Can we get out now?"

The driver rose and unfastened the bubbletop and let the two of them out.

Guards had appeared at the gateway to the palace in the distance.

One of them rushed up. "Dr. Zarkov?" he asked breathlessly. "Good! We've been expecting you."

Zarkov took Dale's arm and helped her down from the heliocab.

"They've been expecting us," Zarkov said, grinning at Dale.

The guards hurried ahead of them, opened the door, and Zarkov and Dale stepped into the outside garden of the palace. A long, wide flight of stairs rose in front of them, and at the top of it, waiting with a smile on his face, stood Prince Barin.

"Prince!" yelled Zarkov. "I haven't seen you in years. How are you?"

Zarkov bounded up the stairs with Dale after him.

Prince Barin reached out and embraced Zarkov in a

big bear hug, his handsome face wreathed in smiles, and his black crew-cut hair now showing a spot or two of gray.

"And Dale," cried Prince Barin, reaching out to embrace and kiss her on the cheek. "Where's Flash?"

Zarkov stared. "They didn't tell you?"

"Tell me what? We got a vidflash that you were on the Great Mongo Desert—I assumed because your rocket had crash-landed, as usual—and I sent out the heliocab to bring you all in."

Zarkov turned to Dale, his face flushed. "I should have been more specific. Flash was captured by Queen Azura's agents, we think," Zarkov said. "We came down right next to the mouth of the Caverna Gigantea."

"But why didn't you come in at the Arboria Jetport?"

"It's a long story," growled Zarkov. "Meanwhile, we've got to get Flash away from Azura."

Prince Barin took a deep breath. "That won't be easy."

"Sure, it will. We just mount a force and wipe them out. You've got the manpower in the Free Council. If you want me to lead them—"

"No way!" Prince Barin said grimly. "I don't think you understand. We've got reports that Azura is joining forces with some secret army to overthrow the whole Free Council of Mongo. And we're not able to do anything about it."

Zarkov stared in stunned astonishment.

Dale stepped forward. "But you've got to save Flash."

Prince Barin's face fell. "I wish we could," he whispered. "But I'm afraid it's impossible."

Chapter 13

In a remote room in the communications tower of Queen Azura's palace sat a bearded young man staring in shock at the vidphone screen in front of him. The image of Azura, the Queen of the Kingdom of Blue Magic, confronted him. He had seen the queen once on the street during a parade, but he had never before been face to face with her, even by remote control.

"You are Jado?" Queen Azura asked brusquely.

"Yes, Your Majesty." She was as beautiful as the legends about her, he decided. But she seemed somewhat older than he had thought. Perhaps the legends exaggerated her youth, if they did not exaggerate her beauty.

"I have a mission for you," she said firmly. "You have been recommended by the minister of communications."

Jado bowed at the torso. "Thank you, Your Majesty, for your trust in me."

"It is a most important mission, Jado—and a dangerous one. Do you think you can handle it?"

Jado stared at the queen's image. Dangerous? Free translation: suicide mission. Jado felt tingles run up and down his backbone. But he did not let his fear show; he had had long training in that. As a courier, he had many times been on impossible missions which depended on bluff and quick wits for survival.

"Absolutely, oh, Your Highness," he said.

"Then come immediately to my chambers; I have a message for you to deliver."

"Yes, Your Majesty," Jado said, bowing once again from the torso.

When he straightened, he saw that the queen's visage had faded from the screen. It was instantly replaced by the frowning face of the minister of communications, an older man named Fraj who thought Jado an upstart and a fool. Jado in turn considered him to be obsolete and senile.

"I've recommended you for a special assignment," Fraj growled at Jado. "I presume the queen has been on the vidphone to you?"

"Yes, sire," said Jado, his lips curling in a mixture of the obsequious and the sardonic. "Thank you, sire."

"Don't thank me," the minister said brusquely. "It's a difficult job. I wish you—uh—godspeed."

"I'm sure you do," Jado said sarcastically, trying to veil his irony.

Minister Fraj did not seem to catch his underling's true meaning, and nodded. "I'll send in a replacement. As soon as he comes, get along to the queen's chambers."

"Thank you," Jado said again, with a wry smile.

The minister faded from the vidscreen and Jado stood up, stroking his beard thoughtfully. He was a young man, in the prime of life, and he was being ordered to do some obviously hazardous deed. He wondered what it was.

Then, chiding himself for his suspicions, he said aloud, "Oh, perhaps it's some personal note to the Free Council of Mongo. In that case, I'll be sent in under the protection of a truce flag. It won't be so bad."

He debated calling his mistress and telling her that he was off on a special mission, but then decided against it. It was strictly forbidden, of course, but all the couriers usually told their wives or mistresses where they would be to avoid personal problems.

Jado stretched and gazed into the mirror, tugging at his beard, and arranging his eyebrows carefully. He was a handsome young man, destined for great things in the hierarchy of the ministry of communications. This might indeed be the mission that could secure him a hold on a higher rung in the ladder of advancement.

He strutted about, waiting for his replacement.

With a hard, strong fist, Jado rapped at the door to the queen's chamber.

"Who is it?" a high-pitched voice cried out. Jado recognized that twisted dwarf's voice—Qilp, wasn't that his name?

"Jado, from the ministry of communications."

"The courier," snapped Qilp, and the door opened immediately. "Hurry up, come on in."

Jado nodded and entered the queen's chamber, looking about him in awe. He took in the long tables, the stairway leading into the upper reaches of the queen's apartment, the slashed remains of the enormous drape that had been cut, for some reason, high at the top of the stairs, and the sight of Queen Azura herself.

Jado bowed sweepingly. "Your Majesty," he said with just the proper deference.

Qilp slammed the door shut and pushed Jado toward the queen, who sat in a comfortable chair not far from the door. She was watching him languorously.

"Come over here, Jado," she said, beckoning with her gloved arm. Jado approached, his eyes gleaming at the sight of her in the tight-fitting sheathlike costume.

Jado stood in front of her. In that position he could see that there were two other men in the chamber. One sat on a large thronelike chair at the side of the room, smiling down at the second man, stripped to the waist, who seemed to be polishing his boots.

An odd scene, Jado thought.

"I have a note for you to deliver, as I said on the vidphone," she told him. Her eyes appraised him shrewdly. "You seem to be a good choice."

"Thank you, Your Majesty," he said.

"Qilp," snapped the queen, "get me the envelope."

"Right," Qilp said, giggling, and ran over to a trestle table nearby. He returned immediately with a sealed envelope and handed it to the queen.

Azura took the envelope and tapped it thoughtfully against a fingernail as she continued to study Jado.

"This is an extremely important message," she told him slowly. "It must be delivered in person to the man to whom it is addressed."

"I understand," Jado said.

"Not really," the queen contradicted him.

Jado waited.

"The message must be delivered and read by the person to whom it is addressed."

"I see. And the person?"

"The addressee is Prince Barin," Queen Azura said softly, "the head of the Free Council of Mongo. He is the ruler of Arboria." A smile tugged at the corners of the queen's beautiful mouth. "It will not be easy to deliver the message, but it must be done."

Jado stared at the queen. "We are not on diplomatic terms with Arboria."

"No, Jado," the queen said.

"I will be seized."

The queen nodded. "Perhaps, yes. If so, we will do everything in our power to have you released, Jado."

Jado sighed. No wonder the minister of communications had selected him: it was a suicide mission.

"I appreciate that, Your Majesty," Jado said wryly.

"I know you do, Jado," Queen Azura responded graciously.

"How can I be sure of even getting to the palace of Prince Barin?" Jado asked.

"That is for you to work out yourself, Jado," the Queen said, her voice hardening. "How you do it is of no concern of mine."

Jado nodded.

She handed the message to him. "Here—take it. No one is to read it but Prince Barin."

Jado bowed. "Thank you, Your Majesty."

"I'm sure," Queen Azura retorted, amused. "Now leave me, please."

Jado turned and hurried to the door. Qilp was there ahead of him, opening it, grinning up with his bright little eyes at Jado.

As Jado left the queen's chambers, he turned in time to see the big man in the chair, whom he thought resembled Ming the Merciless, lean over to slap the face of the blond muscular type man who was polishing the big man's boots.

It was a bad scene, Jado thought, and turned to run down the corridor the moment the door slammed in his face.

What kind of a mission was this?

In his own private rooms, Jado hurriedly unsealed the message with a chemical he kept hidden in his dresser drawer, and opened the sheet of paper.

His face paled.

He would be put to death when this message was read by Prince Barin.

It was a ransom note for the life of Flash Gordon! And the ransom was Prince Barin!

Instantly Jado put two and two together, and realized that the blond man polishing the boots of that look-alike for Ming the Merciless was Flash Gordon, the legendary

Earthman who had helped Prince Barin consolidate the nations of Mongo against the Kingdom of Blue Magic.

Prince Barin would hold Jado hostage—or kill him the moment he fell into their hands.

There had to be someway to deliver the note without putting his own life in jeopardy. He stared out the window a moment, thinking hard.

The gravity sled carried him swiftly through the caverns of the underground world he was familiar with. Jado leaned back and waited for the craft to wind its way through the long tunnels, which had been dug into the lodes of oceanite and which extended through the xanthillium mines even past the boundaries of the Kingdom of Blue Magic into the land claimed by the Kingdom of Arboria.

He glanced down at his attire. He had fitted himself out in the classic uniform of a guard of the forestry security force. As such, he would be able to pass through the cordon of troops surrounding the palace of Prince Barin.

Jado removed the long-handled sharp-bladed knife which he had fitted into his belt. He had been trained in blade-handling during his military days and knew how to use the knife to good effect.

It was fitting that Queen Azura had not told him of the desperate nature of his mission, but had only hinted. She did not want to give specific orders on how to deliver the ransom note. She wanted him to work that out, and he had—in his mind.

She had meant for him to be sacrificed, but he did not intend to be sacrificed. And he would come out of this alive. Was he not Jado, one of the shrewdest in the communications department?

He smiled to himself.

The Azuria miners had penetrated for many hundreds of miles beneath the Great Mongo Desert and beyond the border of Arboria.

Hours after he had started, Jado reached a final mine-shaft marker: "Arboria minus one," it said. He stopped the craft and climbed off into the narrow tunnel that was dimly lighted by converted solar energy.

He walked to the end of the corridor, where stairs ascended in a spiraling corkscrew toward the planet's surface. Jado climbed for some minutes, and finally reached the end of the stairs.

The miners had fashioned exits from the mine that led out through the giant trees that grew above in the forest of Arboria. A wooden ladder had been fastened to the inside of a hollowed-out tree trunk.

Jado climbed up the ladder and came to a door of wood planks which had been fashioned in the side of the tree. He pushed it open. The opening was carefully camouflaged by branches and piles of pine needles.

Jado moved out into the shaded forest and peered around: there was no one in sight. According to the map of the tunnels he had secured from the ministry of mining, he had only a few steps to go through the forest before contacting one of the guard outposts of Arboria.

Quietly, Jado moved through the foliage and finally made out the unmistakable signs of the city up ahead. Then out of the shadows a figure stepped, holding a raygun, and stared at Jado.

"Hold! What is your business outside the city walls?"

Jado smiled. "I have lost my way, Guard. I am one of Prince Barin's forest security detail, out to survey the wood supplies for the winter."

The guard frowned suspiciously, looking more closely at Jado.

"May I see your I.D. card?" he asked.

Jado sighed, and reached into his tunic. He grasped the knife in his belt, brought it out in a smooth and deadly gesture, lunged at the guard, and found his throat with its point before the guard could fire his weapon.

Then he looked quickly around him and saw the tree trunk with the elevator built outside it. He stepped quickly aboard, pulled the rope which initiated the ascension mechanism, and was on his way up to the city.

He was challenged once again on the palace grounds, in the garden under Prince Barin's apartment. The guard asked for his I. D. card and Jado answered with a knife thrust to the heart.

Jado ran in through the entrance and ascended the stairs to the floor where his map showed Prince Barin's rooms to be.

There was no one about, luckily, and he came into the corridor outside the prince's room without attracting any notice. Hearing voices, he paused to listen.

"I tell you, Barin, there has to be a way of mounting an assault force and breaking into the stronghold. If

Flash remains there much longer, I'm sure she'll kill him."

Interesting, thought Jado. He had been right about the blond muscle man. He was Flash Gordon, the great Earthman, hero of Mongo.

Another voice answered, "We have no real proof, Zarkov. You didn't actually see her men take him. And if I send in an assault force, the Free Council will be on my neck for precipitating an incident that might cause intraplanetary war."

"You're much too cautious, Barin," snapped Zarkov. "Now, the way I envision it—"

The two of them leaned closer together, and Jado saw from the doorway that they were huddled together over a table filled with cups and saucers.

Jado glanced up and down the hallway quickly. Barin had been identified by the man called Zarkov. All he had to do was deliver the note.

Quickly, he removed the knife from his belt, shoved the blade through the letter, and moved back into the corridor. In the darkness, he threw the knife, with the note impaled on its blade, into the wall behind the table where the two men were talking.

The knife struck the wall with a thud.

"Look out!" shouted the big bearded man at the table.

"Who's there?" Prince Barin cried, looking over his shoulder into the corridor.

Jado smiled to himself, and ran down the hallway.

Instantly, the palace was in an uproar, but Jado was already on his way down to the unsecured entryway where he had killed the palace guard.

Chapter 14

Prince Barin slowly raised his eyes from the note in his hand. Zarkov saw that his face had lost its color.

"What is it, Barin?" Zarkov asked tensely.

"It's a note from Flash."

Zarkov's eyes widened.

"Flash?"

"Queen Azura is holding him for ransom," Prince Barin said slowly.

Zarkov glowered. "What kind of ransom?"

"Me," Prince Barin said softly, handing the letter over to Zarkov.

"You!" shouted Zarkov. "That's impossible!" He glanced down at the note, reading it in disbelief. "It's not like Flash at all to sound so sniveling, so whining."

Prince Barin moved quickly into a small chamber attached to the royal apartment and flicked on the vidphone.

A face appeared—the thin, no-nonsense, mustached face of a military man.

"Captain Solas," snapped Barin. "Red alert."

"Aye, Prince Barin," Solas replied in the Arboria accent.

"Inform all sentry posts," said Barin. "There is a spy in the city from Azuria, the Kingdom of Blue Magic."

"Aye, that's a serious business," Solas said grimly.

"Block all exits from the city. Stop all strangers. Find him."

Solas nodded. "Aye, sire. . ." And his face faded from the screen.

Prince Barin returned to Zarkov just as Dale Arden entered the room, frowning sleepily. "What's all the excitement about?" she asked. "I was napping, and all of a sudden the palace was in an uproar."

Prince Barin stared at her a moment, but did not answer.

Zarkov looked up from the note with a strained face.

"What is it?" Dale cried, moving rapidly over to Zarkov and grabbing the paper from his hand.

They both studied her in silence as she read the note. "He doesn't sound like himself," she said softly. Her eyes narrowed. "It's that woman," she declared, giving the note to Prince Barin. "She's done something to him." Her eyes brightened. "Drugs?"

Zarkov shook his head. "Hard to tell, but it's Flash's handwriting, and it's his signature." He began pacing. "Well, we aren't getting anywhere just standing here. What are we going to do?" he boomed.

Prince Barin shook his head in annoyance. "There isn't much we can do, Doc."

"But Flash is going to be killed if we don't do something," cried Dale.

"I don't mean we aren't going to do anything, Dale; I simply mean our choices are extremely limited now."

"As if they weren't before," said Zarkov.

"What do you mean?" Dale asked.

Zarkov turned to her. "Prince Barin was holding a meeting of the Free Council before we came to Mongo, Dale. He had not succeeded in moving them to action against Queen Azura, even though there had been some border violations between the Kingdom of Blue Magic and Arboria."

"But now—" Dale began.

"No change," Prince Barin said grimly. "The council is right. Any move will plunge the planet of Mongo into deadly warfare. We would exterminate every living thing. No, I've got to do this thing my way."

Dale folded her arms over her chest. "But meanwhile, what about Flash?" she asked tartly. "Does he stay there in Queen Azura's boudoir—in chains?"

"I'm prepared to act immediately," Prince Barin said.

"Doing what?" Zarkov demanded.

Prince Barin frowned. "The note says if I don't show up alone and unarmed, they'll kill him."

"But you don't intend to—!"

"If Queen Azura ever gets her hands on you, she'll kill you both."

"But I can't just let Flash die without lifting a finger."

The vidscreen glowed with the image of Captain Solas's face. A forest guard immediately outside the city listened as the voice of Solas sounded over the picture.

"All sentry posts!" cried Solas. "Alert for strangers. No one is to leave the city. Do you hear me?"

"Stranger," mused the guard aloud. He had just that moment returned from a short patrol in the woods near the walls of the city. And he had seen. . . .

He ran quickly out into the forest and stared up into the towering trees above him. The elevator was still moving downward, and he saw the man on the elevator platform plainly now. He was dressed in the costume of the Arborian foresters, and yet—

"Halt!" called the guard to the figure on the elevator.

The figure moved quickly, crouching down out of range.

The guard lifted his raygun, set it at stun, and fired quickly at the elevator.

When the elevator reached the bottom of the tree, he ran over and looked down onto the floor of the platform. The raygun had found its mark. The man lay there, unable to move.

The guard hauled him out of the elevator and carried him back tot he outpost where the vidphone was located.

"Captain Solas," he called. "Post fourteen. I think I've got the man you're after."

Captain Solas's image appeared on the vidscreen quickly. "Aye? Where is he now?"

"Right here, sir," said the guard. He lifted the figure so that the face showed on the screen.

"Bring him in," commanded Captain Solas.

"Aye, sir."

Prince Barin paced his room, Zarkov and Dale watching him anxiously.

"We can't let you risk your life," Zarkov announced. "Let me go."

Prince Barin wheeled on Zarkov. "What good would that do, Doc? They want me, not you."

Zarkov pouted. "I could make some kind of bargain with them, couldn't I?"

"I'm the one they're after," Prince Barin insisted. "And I'm the one who has to go."

"But what would happen to the Free Council of Mongo?" Dale asked. "What would happen to Mongo itself? We can't let you go."

"And you'd want Flash dead?" Prince Barin asked, staring bleakly at Dale.

Dale felt tears come to her eyes. "Oh, it's just so awful," she murmured, and turned away so they would not have to watch her cry.

The vidphone buzzed in the next room and Prince Barin rushed out to answer it. In a moment, he returned. "They've got the courier," he said, his face pink with excitement. "They're bringing him up here."

"Maybe we can find out what this is all about," Zarkov growled.

"We already know what it's all about," Prince Barin rejoined, "but maybe we can do a little squeezing."

Dale stared at him blankly. Zarkov's eyes gleamed with anticipation.

In several minutes, Captain Solas approached Prince Barin, accompanied by a dazed but defiant man dressed in Arborian forestry garb.

"Who are you?" Prince Barin asked as the captive was led in.

"A loyal subject, noble Prince Barin," said the forester, bowing at the torso.

Prince Barin turned to Zarkov with a twisted smile. "Well, Doc?"

"Obviously an imposter," Zarkov said firmly. "The accent isn't right at all. And, besides that, he bows at the waist like a subservient vassal of some kind. No Arborian ever does that. This is a democracy."

"The prisoner's face turned slightly pale.

"Well, prisoner," asked Prince Barin, seating himself behind a desk at the end of the room and looking across at his captive, "what do you say to that?"

"I am a loyal subject, Prince Barin," he said again, his eyes betraying tension.

Captain Solas stepped forward. "Prince Barin, this man has killed two of our guards. If you'd like me to take care of him—"

"That won't be necessary," said Prince Barin, holding up a hand. "I'll take care of him myself. You may go, Captain Solas. Leave us, please."

"Aye, sire," Captain Solas said obediently, and about-faced to leave the room.

Prince Barin's face betrayed amusement. "You see, that is the way we do it in Arboria. You have a fairly good disguise in the clothes you wear, but you are not used to our ways here in this free democracy."

The prisoner licked his lips.

Prince Barin's face hardened. "You've killed two of my men. You will be in front of the firing squad within a half hour of your trial. You're caught red-handed."

The prisoner stood rigidly at attention, his eyes fastened on the far wall.

"What's your name?" Prince Barin asked suddenly, in a relaxed voice.

"Jado," said the prisoner after a moment's hesitation.

"Jado," repeated Prince Barin. "Doc?"

Zarkov grinned. "It has the ring of a foreign tongue, Barin," he said loudly. "Jado. I'd guess the Kingdom of Blue Magic. Queen Azura's nether regions."

Prince Barin nodded. "I, too, Doc." His eyes moved back to Jado's face. "Well, Jado?"

Jado's face changed. "I am a loyal subject—" he began.

"But you bow like an Azurian," Zarkov said in a booming, boisterous manner. "How do you account for that?"

Jado straightened. "I deny it."

Prince Barin rubbed his chin. "You're the subject of a foreign power, you've disguised yourself as a civilian, you're prowling about restricted areas, and you're suspected of having killed two guards in Arboria. I don't like to underline the obvious, Jado, but you're in a great deal of trouble."

Jado's eyes shifted to Dr. Zarkov and then to Dale Arden. His lips trembled.

"All right," he said finally. "I am a courier from Queen Azura. As such I demand to be accorded the proper immunity."

"Ah, so he is an Azurian," Zarkov said grimly.

"I come as an official representative of the Kingdom of Blue Magic. I delivered a message to Prince Barin. I deserve immunity."

"But you've killed two men," Prince Barin said darkly. "Do you deny that?"

Jado sucked in his breath. "Sire," he whispered, "I was given a responsible mission by my queen. I had to carry out my duty." His eyes lighted up. "You know there is one of your people involved—a captive of the queen. You understand how necessary it was to deliver the letter intact."

Zarkov smiled crookedly. "Methinks our plucky courier has had a private reading of the note, Barin."

Prince Barin nodded. "He knows his life is forfeit, no matter what."

"I plead immunity," said Jado, by now visibly afflicted with fear.

"No immunity!" snorted Prince Barin. "Where is Flash Gordon?"

"I refuse to divulge military information!" cried Jado.

Prince Barin threw up his hands. "Take him away, Doc. I'll sign the order for his execution."

"You said I would have a trial," Jado cried, scandalized.

"No," said Prince Barin. "Why should we give a trial to someone who does not want to cooperate?"

Jado's mouth twitched. "Cooperate?"

"Yes," Prince Barin said easily. "All we want to know is where Flash Gordon is being held."

"In Queen Azura's palace," Jado said slowly.

"I see," said Prince Barin. Then he shook his head. "We already knew that. No, I'm afraid there'll be no deal—"

Jado leaned forward. "I know more than that. I've seen Flash Gordon. The queen has him drugged and under her control. He's a docile, incompetent coward."

Prince Barin's eyes narrowed. He glanced at Zarkov. Zarkov stared at Jado. Dale turned away and put her hands to her face.

Prince Barin sighed. "I don't know if that will do it or not, Jado. I simply—"

"There's more," said Jado. "I know who the queen is working with. Do you know that?"

"I suppose that you're going to give us that old canard about Queen Azura and the dictators who now rule Mingo."

"She's working with Ming the Merciless, Jr."

Prince Barin's expression did not change. His hands tightened in front of him. "Ming the Merciless is dead," he said softly. "He died without offspring."

"Not true," protested Jado. "I saw Ming the Second at the palace. There have been rumors for a long time, Prince Barin, about a supposed son of Ming. And now—I swear to you—I saw him in the queen's chambers. He was tormenting the stranger."

"The stranger?"

"Flash Gordon," explained Jado.

"Tormenting him?" Zarkov asked.

"I've said enough." Jado stood straight again. "No more."

Prince Barin waved Zarkov away. "We have heard rumors about an exiled son of Ming. You believe that this person you saw was Ming's son?"

"I'm positive about it," Jado said.

"If you're lying, we'll kill you, of course," Prince Barin said easily.

"I do not lie."

Prince Barin nodded silently, and pressed a button on the desk. Instantly, the far door opened and Captain Solas stood there.

"Take him to the counterespionage laboratory, Captain Solas," Prince Barin said.

Captain Solas nodded. "Aye, sire. . . . Come along quickly there, step right along. Hup, two, three, four."

They were gone.

Zarkov leaned on Prince Barin's desk. "Well?"

"Ming the Second," Prince Barin whispered. "Then it is true. Well, that means serious trouble. With Ming's blood line still viable, we've got a bad problem. There are a number of fools on this planet who will follow any demigod. If I don't show up, Queen Azura and Ming the Second will rally both nations to an attack. And that will throw the Free Council of Mongo into complete disarray."

Prince Barin rose, packing back and forth in deep agitation.

"The news about Flash being under the influence of drugs is a sobering thought, indeed. Those scientists of Azuria are far more advanced than our own, although I hate to admit it. They've got him on some kind of fear drug, some pacifist thing, I'm sure. Our own people are trying to work something out, but so far haven't achieved anything more than a couple of fairly ineffective tranquillizers. Oh, well."

Zarkov muttered to himself, tugging at his beard.

"He's probably close to a vegetable," Prince Barin went on. "And that means that he has no way of escaping. We can't depend on him to use his wits and ingenuity to get out of there."

Prince Barin bit his lip.

"How can we get to him?" Zarkov shouted. "I want action, dammit! Not all this standing around and talking."

Prince Barin wheeled on him angrily. "You'll get your action, Doc. It's up to me. I've got to work—and I've got to work fast."

"You insist on going to Queen Azura?" Zarkov asked slowly.

"Yes," replied Prince Barin. He turned to eye Zarkov and a faint smile lightened his grim expression. "But perhaps not exactly the way you think I mean."

Dale looked up. "What have you got up your sleeve, Prince Barin?"

Prince Barin smiled.

Chapter 15

It was a large low-ceilinged room with computer banks standing in rows, tables filled with electronic equipment, and several chairs and complicated scientific measuring devices placed at intervals over the floor space.

Jado was led in by Captain Solas and placed on a bench near the doorway.

"Is this counterespionage?" Jado asked curiously. "It looks more like an experimental lab."

"Just don't worry about it, Jado," Captain Solas said slowly.

In spite of a gnawing curiosity as to what was going to happen to him, Jado relaxed. He thought he had come through the interrogation fairly well. By at first refusing to talk, he had given himself some leeway to bargain with, and when Prince Barin had finally put on the pressure, he had given in a bit to insure his safety. Then when the pressure had been strong, he had given them some imformation that would undoubtedly pay for his life.

Still he was uneasy over what might happen in this room. Queen Azura was the one who supposedly had the best and most gifted scientists on Mongo—but from the looks of it Prince Barin's Arboria lab had every bit as much equipment as she had.

"Do you know what they're going to do to me?" Jado asked. "If it's truth serum, I've already told all I know."

"I have no idea what their plans are for you, Jado," said Captain Solas. "If I were you, I'd consider myself lucky. You've killed two men and you're still alive."

Jado nodded. "I suppose so." He leaned back on the bench.

Soon Prince Barin and Zarkov entered the room. Barin

beckoned to Captain Solas, and the two of them engaged in whispered conversation for a few moments, with Zarkov listening intently.

Then Captain Solas came over and motioned Jado to rise.

"Come on. We're going over to the chair."

Jado began to perspire. He had read in school about that Earth method of putting a person to death—electrocution. Wasn't that done in what was called an "electric chair?"

"You're going to electrocute me?" he whispered anxiously.

Captain Solas smiled grimly. "No Jado. We're not. Although I think even that would be too good for you."

"What's going to happen?" Jado asked in a hoarse voice.

Captain Solas led him to the large metal chair in the middle of the room. In fact, now that he was in the middle of the area, he could see that there were two chairs lined up side by side, almost like the twin thrones of a king and queen.

"Sir down," Captain Solas commanded.

Jado frowned. "I—I don't want to."

"Get in the chair," ordered Captain Solas. He pushed Jado toward the big chair and a guard stepped out from behind a bank of computers and grabbed Jado's other arm.

"I'll go quietly," Jado promised.

He climbed into the chair.

Captain Solas and the guard quickly strapped his chest, arms, and legs to the formidable-looking chair, and stepped away.

Now another figure appeared from the dimness of the computer bank. He was a very obese individual with curly red hair and a benign countenance.

"Major Grof," Prince Barin asked, "are you ready?"

"All ready," Major Grof replied, smiling at Prince Barin and glancing questioningly at Zarkov.

"This is Dr. Zarkov," Prince Barin said, almost as an afterthought.

Major Grof's eyes widened. "I've heard so much about you, Dr. Zarkov."

"I'm sure," said Zarkov, shaking hands. Zarkov's eyes were on Jado. Jado felt cold chills race up and down his spine. For the first time since his capture, he was shaking with fear.

"Well, you've come along to witness the experiment, have you?" Major Grof was gleeful.

"Yes," said Zarkov. "I don't quite understand—"

"It will all be perfectly clear in a moment," Major Grof said, rubbing his hands together. "Perfectly pellucid."

Prince Barin moved over to Major Grof. "How about the prisoner? Is he secured?"

Major Grof nodded, eyeing Jado. Jado stared back at him, feeling the perspiration form on his forehead.

"Get the helmet," ordered Major Grof to the guard who had been helping Captain Solas.

"Aye, sir," said the guard, and hurried off.

Jado tried to see where he was going, but could not follow him.

"Helmet?" Zarkov asked. "What is the helmet for?"

Prince Barin smiled. "You'll see, Doc."

The guard appeared, carrying a large metal helmet that had dozens of wires extending from it. The wires were twisted into a single strand of insulated cord which ended in a metallic jack.

Jado felt his heart jump into his throat. "What is that?"

The guard smiled at him. Major Grof reached out for the helmet and lifted it over Jado's head.

"It's very simple. Just sit there and we'll take care of you. It won't hurt a bit. In fact, you won't feel a thing."

Zarkov was stroking his beard thoughtfully. "What on earth is it, Prince Barin?"

"Ask Major Grof," Prince Barin responded.

Zarkov turned to Major Grof. "Will you tell me now what you're doing?"

"I'm rather busy," Major Grof said pleasantly. He turned to the guard. "Will you get the second helmet, please?"

The guard saluted and ran off.

"Second helmet?" Zarkov repeated, puzzled.

"If you please, Prince Barin," Major Grof said with deference, indicating the second metal chair.

Prince Barin nodded and climbed into the chair.

Zarkov's eyes bulged almost out of his head. "Prince Barin! What is this? Why are you getting into the other chair?"

Prince Barin smiled. "It's perfectly all right. Major

Grof will explain it once we're under the control of the psychescope."

Zarkov's eyes narrowed. "Psychescope?" He glanced at the bank of computers behind the chairs. "That thing?"

Prince Barin nodded. "That's right, Doc."

The guard hurried up with the second metallis helmet, and fitted it carefully over Prince Barin's head. "Is it all right?" he asked anxiously.

"Yes," said Prince Barin. "No discomfort."

"Good," said Major Grof.

He hurried behind the chairs, lifted the two metallic jacks, and inserted both swiftly into corresponding slots in the computers.

Zarkov followed Major Grof behind the chairs and Jado could not see where he had gone. He was staring ahead, his hands trembling on the arms of the metal chair. Somehow knowing that Prince Barin sat in a chair that corresponded to his made him feel somewhat easier, but it did not totally allay his fears of the unknown. What were they doing to him? What were they doing to Prince Barin?

Major Grof came around and stared at Jado. "Are you comfortable?" he asked.

Jado nodded. "Will you please tell me what you're going to do to me?"

"Nothing at all, really," Major Grof said pleasantly. "You'll probably not even experience the slightest discomfort, and you won't remember a thing."

"But—"

"Prince Barin?" Major Grof asked, walking rapidly to stand in front of the other chair.

"Fine," said Prince Barin.

"Good." Major Grof signaled to someone standing in back of Jado's chair. Jado thought it must be Captain Solas, whom he could not see in front of him.

There was a humming whirr in the machinery behind him. Jado moved about inside the helmet, but found that it was quite light and did not wiggle at all. He could feet a pleasant vibration in the top of his skull, and that was all.

In fact, it was so pleasurable that he soon lost all sense of tension and fear. He was very much aware of the room around him, of the table of electronic gear in front of him, of the figure of Dr. Zarkov, who stood in front of him, of Major Grof, who stood by Zarkov and engaged in a whispered conversation with him, of the warm sensation that imbued him from head to foot now. It was like being in a kind of drugged sleep. Pleasurable sensations traveled all through his body. He forgot his travail and thoughts of his mission to Arboria receded into the dim recesses of his mind.

He had a brief glimpse of Queen Azura as he sat there, and thought of his mother for an instant, and his father, and of his tiny apartment in the palace, Then he was back in his childhood briefly, and then he was quite contented to sit in the chair and stare at Zarkov and Major Grof.

He could see a pleasant stream, with a beautiful house surrounded by flowers and lush plants, with the forest in the background. It was familiar, and yet in someway strange to him. He remembered a great deal more then—the beautiful woman who was his mother, the stern man who was his father, the palace and the throne room, and the war in which he rode at the head of the columns of troops, and the celebration when he was proclaimed leader.

The helmet was removed from his head.

"Well?" Major Grof asked, peering at him with deep interest.

"Well, what?" he asked, with a slightly imperious manner.

"Was there any discomfort?"

"None whatever," he replied. "If there had been, I certainly should have complained."

Major Grof smiled. "Good," he said.

"Amazing," said Zarkov, coming around to peer into his face.

"What do you find so amusing, Doc?" he asked.

"It's just that I can't believe what I've seen," Zarkov muttered.

"And what is that?"

"It's as if you've known me for a long time," Zarkov said in awe.

"But we have known each other, Doc, ever since you crash-landed on Mongo six years ago and came to the palace and helped us fight Ming the Merciless. Are you trying to play some kind of joke on me?"

"No," Zarkov said, thoughtfully tugging at his beard. "Not at all."

"All right," said Major Grof. "You can get out of the chair now."

The straps had been loosened by the guard. He got up, stretched, and stood in front of the chair. After a moment, he turned to the second chair nearby. "How's the other one?"

"Fine, fine," said Major Grof.

"Good," he said. "Then you'd better get him out of the helmet."

"Aye," said Major Grof.

He held up a hand. "Wait—how long do you think it will be before Jado can leave for the Kingdom of Blue Magic?" he asked.

An amused Major Grof said, "Right away."

"So be it," said Prince Barin.

To Zarkov the whole proposition had been one of the most amazing performances he could remember.

Jado, the prisoner, and Prince Barin were strapped to adjoining metal chairs, helmeted and hooked up to the computer bank, with Major Grof behind them working at the dials and switches.

When finally the major had finished, he stood by Zarkov, and Zarkov had asked him what was happening.

"It's personality transference," Major Grof said in a whisper. "It's forced extrasensory perception, actually. The computers are wired to promote maximum power. Then the memory of the prisoner from Azuria is slowly erased from his mind by means of the psychescope to which he is wired."

"Like shock therapy?" Zarkov asked eagerly.

"Essentially, but without the disorientation and the danger of permanent amnesia. The memory is simply wiped clean in moments, as the sweep washes out the subject's memory bank from present to past, leaving it completely blank. Then, taking the memory of the other subject, the psychescope force-feeds it into the blank memory bank so that Subject A has the memory and personality of Subject B. And, meanwhile, Subject B takes on the memory and personality of Subject A."

"Then you mean that Prince Barin will actually take on the prisoner's personality?"

"Exactly," Major Grof said, beaming.

"And the prisoner will become Prince Barin?"

"Right." Major Grof added: "But that's not quite all.

Although the prisoner will be locked into the personality and memory of Prince Barin, that is, he will be Prince Barin for all intents and purposes and no one else, Prince Barin will take on the personality and memory of Jado, but will also retain his entire memory himself so that he is both Prince Barin and Jado."

"Fascinating," muttered Zarkov. "Forced schizophrenia! You think it will work?"

"It will," said Major Grof.

And it had. Minutes later, Jado had emerged from under the helmet and stepped off the metal chair, thinking he was Prince Barin.

"Captain Solas," commanded Major Grof. "Please take—uh—the prince into the cosmetology room."

Captain Solas hurried over and led the erect figure from the room into an adjoining one.

"Well, he certainly passed the test," Zarkov admitted. "Where did Captain Solas take him?"

"To the cosmetology room," said Major Grof.

"I don't think I understand." Zarkov blinked. "Yes, I get it! For cosmetology transference, to correspond to the personality transference."

"Exactly, so that Jado will look like Prince Barin."

"And Barin?"

Major Grof waved at the other chair. "Ask him."

Zarkov strode over to the chair and waited while Major Grof lifted off the helmet.

"How did it go, Prince Barin?"

Barin laughed. "Fine, fine, Major. You've never given me any trouble yet, have you?"

"Where were you born, Jado?" asked Major Grof.

"In the Kingdom of Blue Magic," Barin answered in the voice of Jado.

Zarkov blinked. "Incredible."

"Who sent you here?"

"Queen Azura."

"Was Flash Gordon indeed in that room with Ming the Second?" Zarkov asked.

"Yes," Barin said in Jado's voice. "I saw the two of them."

Major Grof nodded. "Good, good."

"Now what, Barin?" asked Zarkov.

Prince Barin laughed. "To the cosmetology room. Right, Major Grof?"

"Right."

Zarkov beamed. "So you'll look like Jado."

"You're a bright fellow, Doc. You should take up science."

Zarkov glowered. "Come off it, Barin. That's not funny."

Prince Barin roared with laughter.

Chapter 16

Queen Azura leaned back on the silken coverlet of the banquette by the great dining table and surveyed Ming the Second through lidded eyes. The son of Ming the Merciless was flushed with wine, sluggish with a great deal of food, and quite unable to utter a word without slurring it.

"Soon!" he shouted. "Soon we will rule this whole planet, you and I, Queen Azura." He threw back his head and laughed uproariously, reaching out for another flagon of wine which he gulped down quickly.

Azura stifled a yawn. "Yes, Ming. Now, darling, if you'rc quict through eating, perhaps you should go to bed. You need rest, you know. Prince Barin may be coming any hour now. I wouldn't want his visit to be marred by any lack of vigilance on your part, my dearest one."

Ming stared at her, his eyes unable to focus. "Oh, the hell with Barin, love. We'll take care of him with no trouble at all. After all, once he's in our hands"—he grinned and slashed his forefinger across his neck—"it's off with both their heads." He roared with laughter.

"You drunken sot," Queen Azura said under her breath. "What ever gave me confidence in you as a military ally?"

"What's that, Queen?" Ming asked, his head lolling forward. "Wha' you say?"

"Never mind, darling," said Azura, reaching out her hand commandingly. "I do think you had better retire, love. It's going to be a busy day."

"Busy night," Ming said, chuckling, getting up from the chair and staggering around the table toward Azura.

Azura rose to her feet in a regal manner, standing straight and tall. "Get out of here, Ming, or I'll call Qilp."

Ming grabbed her by the arms. "What can stupid Qilp do to me, 'Zura?" he muttered.

She moved quickly, slapping him in the face. "Get away from me, Ming," she ordered. "You're totally drunk. Get to bed and sleep it off before you touch me."

Standing back in awe, feeling his face with his hand, Ming blinked and suddenly focused on her. "Hey, you hellcat, what do you think you're doing? This is Ming, baby. Not some stupid courtier you fancy."

Azura clapped her hands in command and moved quickly away from Ming.

He came after her, reaching out and grabbing the thin cape she wore over her shoulder. It ripped and fell to the stone floor.

The door opened and Qilp ran in. He carried an enormous leather-thonged whip in his hands.

Azura said nothing, but threw her hand toward Ming, who was stumbling after her, pawing at her. Qilp's eyes gleamed and he flicked the whip quickly so that the thongs caught Ming in the back of the neck.

He yelled in pain, reaching his hand behind his neck. He whirled, and saw the dwarf coiling the whip for another strike. He roared and jumped for the dwarf.

The little man was as agile as a rabbit, and jumped out of the way, running back along the wall, with the whip ready.

"I'll get you, you deformed little monster!" shouted Ming, and reached out his hands again. "Cousin or no cousin."

Azura walked sedately out of the dining room and into her own chamber. She slammed the door and locked it.

There was another animal-like roar from Ming. She studied herself in the mirror and smiled slightly as she heard the heavy blows raining upon the thick door, and the outraged cries of Ming the Second.

"Let me in, will you? What kind of treatment is that, Azura? Come on, baby, I was only playing."

"You've had a busy day, little man," Azura said distinctly through the door. "Better get some rest. Tomorrow you meet Prince Barin."

Azura leaned forward, staring into her eyes in the mirror. She was sick and tired of Ming and his adolescent interest in athletics and games. Had she made a mistake in hiding him in Azuria while he grew to manhood, so she could use him to conquer the entire planet? Should she perhaps have chosen some other man to be her king?

She shrugged.

It was too late now to make any changes. If only Ming were like Flash Gordon, now. But, of course, he was not.

There was a discreet rap on the door fifteen minutes later.

"Who is it?" Azura asked from the silken-draped bed upon which she lay, fully dressed, reading a book.

"Jado, Your Majesty."

"Oh, the courier!"

She rose and quickly unlocked the door.

The man she recognized as the courier to whom she had given the note for Prince Barin stood before her, looking down into her eyes.

"Come in," she said softly, and Jado stepped inside the room. She pushed the door shut behind him and walked slowly to the bed, where she sat down, leaning back against the bolster.

"Well?" she said softly.

Jado came over and stood by the bed. "The message was delivered, Your Majesty."

"How can I believe that?" she asked.

Jado smiled. His eyes were appraising her. "You can believe it, Your Majesty, because I say it. Did you take me for a fool?"

"How a fool?"

"If I had delivered the letter as you told me to, without knowing the contents, I would have been seized and thrust into prison in Arboria."

The queen smiled. "And?"

"I saw that the note was delivered to the proper person, and then made my escape, Your Majesty," Jado said sardonically. He bowed stiffly at the torso.

"You amuse me, Jado. Perhaps you are not the fool I took you for."

"Indeed I am not," Jado said with a faint smile.

"And Prince Barin?"

"He has the message. He will come."

"You are sure?"

"Your Majesty, because I did apprehend the contents of the message, and because I did realize what you wanted, I simply made sure I overheard the discussion that followed the rather dramatic reception of the note."

The queen chuckled. "You are one of a kind, Jado."

"He is coming in the early morning—overland through the Great Mongo Desert."

"Excellent, Jado. Excellent. Alone?"

"He debated that for some time with his ministers," Jado continued, his eyes narrowed. "They finally decided that he must obey the tenor of the note in order to be in a position to save his friend Flash Gordon."

"I see," said the Queen. "And how does he intend to do that?"

"I do not know," said Jado.

"Then we will secure him the moment he appears," said the queen.

Jado bowed at the waist.

"Jado," said the Queen. "How did you return?"

"From Arboria?" Jado asked with a frown.

"Yes."

"The same way I went, Your Majesty."

"Through the Great Mongo Desert?" the Queen asked negligently.

"No, Your Majesty. Through the labyrinth of tunnels in the mining sector of the Caverna Gigantea."

"Ah," said the Queen. "Ingenious."

"Yes, Queen Azura."

"What did the Arborians say to you, Jado?"

"They said to halt, and I killed one of them," Jado replied with a faint smile.

"I mean in the court?"

"I spoke to no one," Jado replied stiffly.

The queen nodded slightly. "What is our minister of communication's name, Jado?"

"Fraj, Your Majesty," Jado said with an amused smile.

The Queen laughed. "I am eternally suspicious of Arborians, Jado. I am simply testing you to see that you have not been programmed to give me the right answers after having been brainwashed—or possibly having been killed and a spy sent in your place."

Jado's eyes were bright. "An amusing concept, Your Majesty."

"Is it not?" the queen responded.

"Have I passed the test, Your Majesty?"

"For the time being, Jado," the queen said serenely. "You may go."

Jado nodded and bowed again.

"I like you, Jado," the queen said quite suddenly. "I

plan to reward you for your faithful mission. Remain nearby so I can summon you."

"Yes, Your Majesty." Jado smiled into her eyes.

Queen Azura reached out her hand and touched his cheek. "Leave me, Jado."

He bowed and walked slowly out of the queen's bedchamber.

The queen lay there a moment, bemused. Jado was a bright young man, certainly. He had proved quite shrewd in his actions so far; perhaps she could use him.

She looked at the ceiling of her chamber. Perhaps he was too bright. Perhaps he had proved his worth to her only to make himself visible for further advancement, and then turn against her.

There were always courtiers plotting against her, she knew. And Ming—how could he take to Jado?

The thought of the two of them at each other's throats amused her.

She would keep a close eye on Jado. Perhaps she could use him yet if she ever parted ways with Ming.

On the other hand, he could have been suborned by Prince Barin. Jado could be an agent of the Arborians. Their scientists were as ingenious as her own. Yes, she would keep an eye on Jado.

She reached out and flicked on the vidphone.

"Ming," she hissed, and the screen cleared. She saw Ming's bloated flushed face.

"Hey!" Ming exclaimed. "What did you wake me up for?"

"The outpost, fool," snapped Azura. "Prince Barin is on his way. Over the Great Mongo Desert."

"You're lying," growled Ming. "Let me sleep."

"Get your troops out there and wait for him," ordered Azura. "Or I'll throw you in the dungeons."

"Aw, now," growled Ming in a nasty way, "get off my back, will you?"

"Move," Azura demanded angrily. "Or I'll have you in irons!"

"Yes, oh, queen," snarled Ming, his eyes black with anger and hate.

Chapter 17

Just inside the mouth of the cave where the Caverna Gigantea opened out onto the cliff face of oceanite rock, Ming the Second waited with a group of Azurian guards in full regalia. It was almost dawn.

The vidphone sounded and Ming turned to it, cursing the headache that still plagued him after all those hours. Queen Azura's face came into focus on the vidscreen.

"Ming!" she snapped. "Where are you?"

"Here, oh, queen," Ming said with a growl.

"We've calculated Prince Barin's journey across the Great Mongo Desert. He should be there before the sun rises. Can you see him now?"

"Not now, but we are watching."

"Good—keep at it."

Ming scowled at the vidscreen as the queen's visage faded. Damned meddling woman, he thought. It had been a mistake to let her lead him all the time. He should have fled Azuria when a youth and returned to Mingo. There he could have built up an army of his own to overthrow the caretaker government and set himself up as emperor. He could have gotten followers to help him.

But he had chosen to let Queen Azura talk him into joining forces with her. The trouble was the queen herself. She was an egotistical, vain, and rather stupid woman. She thought she was a great deal smarter than she was. And she loved to throw her power around, particularly to make a man look stupid. In spite of all her attempts, he knew that he did not look as stupid as some of her courtiers. Take that dwarf, for example, his cousin.

Yet Qilp, even though a blood relation, was to be avoided as much as possible. He was a dangerous little sneak. A spy. A deadly agent. A murderer. All those things. But someday. . . .

Ming had the shakes from the enormous amount of alcohol he had consumed the night before. It was going to be one of those days, he thought miserably.

"Ming," said one of the guards, pointing out through the entranceway of the cave.

Ming rose and looked over the guard's shoulder. In the distance they both saw the tiny figure of a man walking through the bolder-strewn passageway.

"Prince Barin," said Ming, unable to identify the man from the distance, but quite sure who it was.

"He's bearing a white flag," announced another guard.

Ming nodded, a smile twisting his mouth. "Good. He's following his orders, so far. Now we wait."

"Wait, Ming?"

"Wait, to see if he has brought along any other hidden men to help him, fool!" said Ming.

"Yes, Ming," said the guard.

"Then, when we are sure there is no one to help him, we seize him."

The guards waited silently, while Ming paced back and forth inside the cave. After a few minutes, Ming looked out and saw Prince Barin there, standing with the flag beside him.

"Azurians!" a faint voice called from below. "I am Prince Barin, come to surrender to you."

Ming rose and peered out into the dawn light which was just beginning to break.

"Are you alone?"

"I am alone," Prince Barin responded.

"Approach, Prince Barin," Ming said, hiding a contemptuous smile.

The figure moved toward them through the boulders and loose dirt.

When Prince Barin was at the entrance to the cave, the guards sprang out and grasped him from both sides.

"Here, what is this?" Prince Barin asked.

"See if he is armed," commanded Ming.

The guards frisked him.

"No weapons, Ming."

"All right," said Prince Barin. "So it is Ming the Second, isn't it? We had heard rumors about you. You're working with Queen Azura?"

"Indeed I am," said Ming. "The rumors are true."

"Well, then, you've got me. Now fulfill your bargain, and let Flash Gordon go."

Ming threw back his head and burst into laughter. "Bargain? Idiot! Do you expect to bargain with an emperor?"

"What?" Prince Barin muttered. "You're not an emperor."

"No? I'll take you and Flash and a thousand more troops in payment for the throne you have robbed me of!"

"It was your father who lost the throne, Ming, not you." Prince Barin tried to pull away from the guards. "You've got to let me go. A bargain is a bargain."

"An emperor doesn't make bargains with underlings," Ming said contemptuously.

Prince Barin struggled again, breaking loose from one of the guards. He swung his fist at Ming's face. In frenzied reaction, Ming twisted the raygun out of his belt and smashed Prince Barin's face with the barrel.

Prince Barin screamed and fell back into the hands of the guards.

"That'll teach you to play games with me!" Ming yelled. He turned to the guards, his face grim. "Bind him up and let's get him out of here. I don't trust him, anyway. He might have his own troops hiding out there. Hurry it up, you clods."

Ming flicked on the switch of the vidphone.

"Queen Azura," he called.

Her face faded in. "Yes, Ming?"

"We've got him," Ming said, allowing himself a satisfied grin. "He walked right into our trap."

"Good," Azura said heartily. "Now bring him to the palace and we'll put the rest of the plan into action."

"Yes, Your Majesty," said Ming as he bowed and snapped off the vidphone.

His eyes narrowed. He wondered if he could trust the queen. She said she was going to kill Flash Gordon, but Ming knew that she had once been in love with him. He wondered if perhaps her scheming little mind might not be planning some other kind of trick—like a double cross.

Take Flash Gordon as her king.

And kill Ming the Second.

Nasty little minx—he would have to cross that bridge when he came to it. Thoughtfully, he turned to watch the guards carrying Prince Barin into the corridor that opened out into the Caverna Gigantea.

The dungeon chambers lay directly below Queen Azura's chambers in the palace of Azuria. The stone walls were as thick as the height of a man, with small, high windows barred with duroplast, Mongo's strongest steel substitute.

The torture chambers were off to one side of the dungeons. From the walls hung chains with wrist manacles at their ends, and leg irons screwed into the rock walls. A rack was mounted in one corner, operated by a small computer to one side of it. Ropes and chains hung from the ceiling, where prisoners could be suspended, their feet barely touching the floor.

There were several variations of the iron maiden, and a long bench of thumb screws, wrist puncturers, and evisceration machines for special cases of recalcitrancy.

Ming followed the guards into the torture chamber and watched as they lifted Prince Barin into the air and locked the manacles to his wrists, so that he hung from chains screwed into the ceiling.

When they pulled away a long work ladder, Prince Barin sank down toward the floor, his arms high above his head, and his wrists already white from lack of blood.

Ming smiled with satisfaction.

He sauntered over to the dangling figure of the ruler of Arboria.

"Prince," Ming said with a fiendish smile. "Now you know how it feels to be without a kingdom. Now you know how I feel—how I felt all during the years I was growing up."

Prince Barin grimaced. "Cut me down, Ming. This isn't fair. I made a bargain."

"Fair? Unfair? Words, Prince Barin," scoffed Ming. "Possession is nine tenths of the law. And we possess you. We also possess Flash Gordon. Now we own both of you. And we wouldn't let you go, no matter what ransom was paid us. The Free Council has no leader like you. They'll fold up quicker than a house of cards when we attack." Ming laughed. "And I'll be ruler of the kingdom that was stolen from my father."

Prince Barin blinked. "It was not stolen. The people revolted against the tyranny of your late father. They simply threw off the yoke of repression and opted for freedom. Be sensible, Ming. If you undertake to treat them the way your father did, they'll throw you out, too."

"Not me," said Ming. "I've read the histories. My father was a fool, counseled by idiots and blunderers. His armies were full of cowardly generals. I'll lead them like a man should. I'll be the greatest emperor the planet Mongo has ever known."

"You're a fool, Ming," Prince Barin replied, and grimaced as pain shot through his arms.

"Fool!" cried Ming. He turned to the guards. "Leave him there. Meanwhile, I'm going to take care of Flash Gordon."

There was a sudden silence in the chambers. A door clanged shut.

Ming wheeled around.

Queen Azura stood there with Qilp beside her. She was scowling at Ming.

"Getting your kicks, Ming?" she asked with a sneer. "I told you to imprison him, not torture him."

Ming stood taller and strolled over to her, his face hard. "What's the difference, oh, Queen Azura?" he asked with a snarl. "I'm getting sick and tired of having to follow all your orders point by point. This man Barin is responsible for the fact that I was exiled from my home and betrayed by my kingdom."

"Your father disowned you," Azura said testily. "If anyone is to be blamed, it is he, not Prince Barin."

Ming's vision turned a blurry red. He stalked toward the queen. "There's no reason for us to quarrel," he said in a threatening voice. "We've got Flash Gordon and Prince Barin both in our hands. What does it matter what we do with them? We can kill them or we can torture them. Anything we do now will be all right. We simply have to inform the Free Council that Prince Barin is in our hands, and we can take over control without even using our troops."

Azura stared up at him. "You leave them both alone, understand?"

"You still fancy the Earthman, don't you, Your Majesty?" asked Ming, leaning over the queen. "That's why you don't want me to touch him, because I'll spoil your fun." Ming roared with laughter.

Azura stared at him with loathing.

"All right," Ming said finally. "I'll promise you not to touch your beloved. You can do with him what you will. I don't care. You can even keep him around as a pet while we rule Mongo together."

"Shut up, you monster!" screamed Azura. "It's a matter of policy I'm talking about. Not passion. You're a dull-witted fool, Ming. Now get out of here and leave these hostages alone. I've got plans for them."

Ming stared. "I'll just bet you have, my beloved queen," he said, chuckling. "I'll just bet you have."

Azura drew back her hand to slap Ming's face, then thought better of it.

"Get out of here," she told him in a low voice. "Guards! Leave me, please. Take your leader with you." She glowered at Ming.

Ming straightened. "Let's go, men. Queen Azura is not amused." He smiled at her as he left and turned to Prince Barin, who dangled helplessly from the ceiling. "She's all yours, Prince Barin."

His laughter echoing in the torture chamber, Ming and the guards departed.

Queen Azura stared at Prince Barin for a moment, and then turned away from him. Her face was white with rage.

"Your Majesty," Prince Barin said hoarsely as he twisted his wrists in the shackles.

She spun on her heel and frowned. "Yes?"

"You've got to let Flash Gordon go. It's part of our bargain."

Queen Azura stared at him and suddenly her face stiffened. She looked back at the door through which Ming and the guards had left.

"Bargains are made to be broken," she said thoughtfully. A small smile spread across her beautiful lips. She began laughing. "All bargains. . . ."

Chapter 18

Giving himself a passing glance in one of the palace mirrors, Prince Barin was astonished at the complete disguise the cosmetologists in Arboria had given him. He looked absolutely like Jado, the Azurian courier.

It was a lucky break for him that Queen Azura had become interested in Jado, enough to invite him to remain near the royal chambers. He had called in to Fraj, the minister of communications, by vidphone and told him of the queen's orders.

Then he had begun to roam about the premises. What he needed, of course, he did not know where to find. However, since he knew it must be in the scientific laboratories, he tried to locate it there first.

The labs were in the central part of the palace in a wing adjacent to the queen's apartment. The scientists in Azuria were held in high esteem and occupied four floors.

Prince Barin had already explored one of them without finding what he wanted. The first floor he had visited was involved with military travel—vehicles for personnel, vehicles for arms, and so on. It was the scientific-formulation section he was after.

Now, arriving at the second floor of the scientific sector, Prince Barin nodded to one of the security men on duty, flashed Jado's I.D., and moved on through the door.

Here he could see long rows of tables covered with test tubes, and other lab paraphernalia. He felt his heartbeat quicken.

Two bespectacled scientists glanced up and nodded at him as he hastened past with a cheery wave of the hand. There were drawers and cupboards along one long wall, and it was at these that Prince Barin paused, glancing up and down the long counter as if he were looking for something that had been removed from his sight.

Surreptitiously he studied the labels on the drawers.

NC17G NER
CN5 PAC
KE98 ROC PRO
FM116 EXP
JG34 NER

And so on.

Prince Barin frowned. "Ner." Nerve gas? Quite probably. "Pac." What? "Roc Pro" was most certainly rocket propellant. And "Exp" was explosives.

"PAC"—pacifist gas?

Prince Barin glanced up and down the counter, but no one was in sight.

He reached out and flung open one of the cupboard doors. Inside he scrutinized a row of jars and bottles. Each had a label pasted to the outside—CN5, CN6, CN13.

He lifted one down and studied it more closely.

This could be what he was looking for. He remembered the formulation code: CN and whatever number followed.

Then he put the jar back, closed the door, and went on down the line.

At the end, he came to a cabinet with the letters "CAP 5NC."

Something rang a bell.

He paused, and flipped the door open.

A row of jars stood there. He took one down and studied it closely. CAP 5NC; backward it was CN5 PAC. Backward because this was the antidote to the original drug?

Prince Barin slipped the jar into his pocket and closed the door quickly. One of the scientists was walking rapidly toward him.

He turned, smiled, and pushed past, making for the door into the lab.

As he reached out to open it, he was surprised to see it move quickly toward him as someone from outside moved rapidly in.

Queen Azura!

She stared at him in instant recognition.

"Jado," she said. "My courier. What are you doing down here?"

"You said to be available, Your Highness," Prince Barin said in Jado's voice, bowing at the waist.

The queen's expression softened. "Yes, I did suggest that, didn't I?" Her eyes narrowed. "I hadn't expected you to take my suggestion literally, however. I had simply meant for you to be on call. You are interested in laboratory work?"

"In a minor way, Your Majesty," Prince Barin said, turning slightly to hide the bulge in his tunic.

"It is always fascinating work," she said softly. "Since you are here, perhaps you can help me in one of my projects."

"Certainly, Your Majesty," Prince Barin said, feeling a very strong urge to bolt and run for safety.

"Come with me," said the queen, and led him through the counters of beakers and test tubes to the far wall, where Prince Barin had explored the shelves already.

Unerringly, the queen took him to the cabinet in which he had seen the CN5 PAC jars. She reached up and took one down. Her eyes were amused.

"It is time for the prisoners to eat dinner, Jado. Perhaps you could help me feed them."

"Certainly," Prince Barin said softly.

"You know how to fix the food of Flash Gordon?" Queen Azura asked with a smile.

"I can certainly guess, Your Majesty," Prince Barin said, smiling at the jar in the queen's hand.

"Yes. It is a drug that makes a man a coward, Jado. Mixed with his food, he cannot taste nor smell it, yet when he has finished eating, he is a mouse." She laughed softly.

"Ah-ha!" Prince Barin said in Jado's voice, smiling slyly. "So that is how the Earthling has been made so docile. I had heard that Ming the Second has been having sport with the Earth hero."

Queen Azura's face hardened. "Yes, Ming has been taunting the prisoner. I am not sure I like that, but there is probably no harm done." She looked at him. "You will feed the Earthling?"

"Of course, Your Majesty. I shall fix his food for him."

"Do not tarry in the prisoner's cell," Queen Azura warned him. "It can be dangerous."

"I shall obey."

Queen Azura led Prince Barin out through the tables

of test tubes and Bunsen burners and into the corridor. "Serve me well and I will not forget you, Jado."

"I act on your command, Queen Azura."

Azura smiled briefly, and moved away down the corridor toward her apartment. Prince Barin went the opposite way, down a winding stairway toward the dungeon chambers.

In the corridor outside the dungeons, Prince Barin met one of the prison guards wheeling a tray of food.

"Guard," said Prince Barin in Jado's voice, "the Queen commands that I feed the prisoner Flash Gordon. Can you lead me to his cell?"

"Certainly," said the guard, after looking at Jado's I.D. "This way."

Prince Barin followed the guard with the serving table around a corner and down four cells. The door before which the guard paused was bigger than most, with a tiny barred window in the planking.

"All right, Guard," said Prince Barin. "Leave me the tray. I'll take it in."

"Aye, aye," muttered the guard, bowing. He moved off down the corridor.

Prince Barin glanced around quickly, removed the jar of CAP 5NC from his tunic, poured some of it in the plate on the tray, and quickly put the jar away. Then he took the food cart, lifted the latch on the outside of the huge door, and pushed inside the cell.

It was dark in the cell, illuminated only by a tiny glow of light in the high ceiling. It took Prince Barin a moment for his eyes to grow accustomed to the subdued illumination in the small room.

"Who is it?" a pitiful voice asked from the corner.

Prince Barin was shocked at the sound of Flash Gordon's voice. It was Flash all right. He knew the familiar tones, but he could not believe the pitiful quality that seemed to infect the voice itself.

He could see him now, stripped to his powerful waist, his huge shoulders visible, naked and muscled, with the slacks and military boots scratched and dirty. The big man was cringing in the corner, trying to get away from Prince Barin, whom he obviously considered another threat. He was like a mouse!

"What do you want?" Flash whined piteously.

I wish I could tell you, Flash, Barin thought. It would

help ease your ordeal. But not now, my good friend. Not till it's time to make them cringe.

"I've brought you some food, Earthling," Prince Barin said in the tones of Jado. "Here. Eat heartily! Maybe it will make a man out of you." Jado roared with mirth.

"I don't think I'm hungry," Flash said in a whisper. "I don't feel like eating."

Prince Barin swaggered dorward toward his friend. "Eat that food, you lout, or I'll pound it down your throat."

Flash hung his head. "Please, please!"

"Are you going to eat?" yelled Prince Barin. "Or do I have to chew it for you?"

"All right," whispered Flash. "I'll eat. Don't get mad at me."

Prince Barin held the food out to Flash, and muttered darkly, "Sorry, old friend. I wish I could tell you this is your comrade Barin and that I'm here to help you, but I've got to be sure that antidote works."

"How do you like it, coward?" cried Prince Barin in Jado's voice. "Is it good?"

"Oh, it's very, very good," said Flash.

"I'll tell the queen. She will be delighted," Prince Barin said sarcastically.

"Queen Azura?" Flash repeated, dazed.

"Yes," Prince Barin said, laughing. "Isn't she a beautiful woman, Earthling?"

"Oh, yes," said Flash, putting down his empty plate. "There. You can take it all away now. I've eaten."

"Good for you," growled Prince Barin. "You've licked the platter clean!"

"Yes," Flash said with a smile.

Prince Barin gathered the empty plates together and put them on the server. He pushed it to the door, opened it, and was about to wheel it out into the corridor when someone moved quickly to his side.

He glanced up, startled.

It was Queen Azura.

Her eyes narrowed in suspicion. "Still here, Jado? I didn't tell you to spoon-feed him. I simply told you to administer the drug to his food. You work very slowly."

Prince Barin bowed as Jado might, his eyes avoiding hers. He could tell she was annoyed at the fact he had seen her. He could also tell that she was suspicious of him now. He had lingered too long.

But why was she visiting Flash? What was behind the

visit that she so obviously wanted kept secret? Something was afoot; Prince Barin did not like it at all.

Queen Azura drew herself up. "I wish to be alone with the prisoner," she said firmly. "Let no one enter the dungeons, Jado. Not even Ming himself, should he try."

"The great Ming?" Prince Barin repeated.

"Yes." The queen glanced up and down the corridor. "Now go, and guard the end of the corridor. You hear me?"

"I hear and I obey, Your Highness."

Prince Barin pushed the server out of the way and hastened down the corridor to the end where the locked door kept it isolated from the other parts of the dungeon.

He could hear the door squeak open behind him as Queen Azura entered Flash Gordon's cell.

Alone with the prisoner," Prince Barin thought. That could be dangerous. What if the antidote takes effect while she's there? She'll know that I gave it to him! I've got to work fast.

He shrugged helplessly. But how? Shaking his head, Prince Barin quickly secured the door to the corridor, and stood by it, his arms folded over his chest.

Was Azura going in there to kill Flash Gordon? Was that part of the bargain?

For Ming's sake?

Yet she had said not to let even Ming in, should he try.

Prince Barin shuddered.

"I hope that antidote doesn't take effect and tip off the queen," he said aloud.

He felt suddenly cold in the corridor and shivered. He wished he knew what was happening inside the cell.

Chapter 19

Queen Azura gazed at Jado's retreating back and frowned.

Too bad, she thought. No one must know of my visit to Flash Gordon. Word of it would get immediately to Ming. And I don't like to think what he might do about it.

She sighed.

So Jado must die to protect the secrets he knows. And I wonder what took him so long with Flash Gordon.

She turned and pushed her way into Flash's cell, using the master key she carried to all doors in the palace.

Flash was cringing in the corner, still unnerved from the visit of Jado.

"Don't pull away from me, Flash," she said in a soothing voice, and walked over to the corner where he was hiding.

He scrambled against the wall, trying to get away from her.

She reached out a hand to touch his naked shoulder. "Don't be afraid of me," she whispered. "I'm your friend."

Flash turned and stared at her vacantly. "You're the queen," he said.

"Yes," said Azura. "No one must know of this visit. I've come to talk to you, Flash."

"I don't want to talk," Flash said, and turned his face to the wall.

"Please," said Azura. "Talk to me."

Finally Flash made up his mind. He turned toward her. "All right," he said softly.

"That's better," said Queen Azura.

She stared at his huge shoulder muscles and his enormous chest. She could not help but compare his build to that of Ming's. And she found Ming wanting.

"We have known each other a long time, Flash," she said ingratiatingly.

"Yes, Queen Azura," Flash said dutifully.

"Things have not really changed between us," she added thoughtfully.

"How do you mean?"

"I have always felt that even though you pretend not to like me, you do," the Queen said softly.

"Perhaps," Flash said doubtfully.

"I mean there is more than 'like' there, Flash! When first we met, I thought we would spend the rest of our lives together."

"Oh," said Flash.

Azura felt a sudden anger at his obvious reluctance to talk about her feelings for him. She tried to hold her annoyance in check.

"Time has passed, Flash, but I find that I feel exactly the same about you as I once did." She sank down next to him, barely touching him.

He stirred. "That's interesting," he said.

"Interesting!" she repeated. "What kind of a man are you? I'm talking about love—I'm talking about how I feel for you. Are you made of concrete?"

Flash shook his head. He was watching her. For some odd reason, she sensed a difference in him, but she could not analyze it.

"I am queen of the most advanced civilization on Mongo," she said proudly. "The Azurian."

Flash nodded.

"For some time now I have been preparing to take a king."

There was silence.

"But the man I have chosen is not good enough to be King of Azuria," she whispered.

She moved closer to him.

"I want you."

Flash stared at her coldly. "You have always been an enemy of my friends on Mongo," Flash said unhappily.

His defiance surprised her a bit, but she did not pause. "But that is easily rectified."

"Then let Prince Barin go."

Azura was at a loss for words.

Then she spoke. "If I let Prince Barin go, will you take me—and my kingdom—for yours?"

Flash Gordon stared at her for a long moment. He did

not seem to be trembling as much as before. She wondered vaguely if the pacifist mist might not be wearing a bit thin.

But no—it was much too powerful to wear off in twenty-four hours.

"If you let him go and I can see him go free," Flash said slowly, "then perhaps."

"No!" she snapped, unable to control her temper. "We will marry first and then Prince Barin will go free."

Flash shook his head. "Then I will not accept."

She leaped to her feet, balling her hands into fists at her sides. She was seething with anger.

"You fool! Why are you so stubborn? What is wrong with me? Am I ugly? Am I deformed? Don't you know I am the most beautiful woman on Mongo?"

Flash smiled faintly, looking up at her.

"I'll have you killed if you don't accept my offer!" she railed. "I'll have you put to death."

Flash stood slowly. "You're beautiful. I'm not blind. But I can't marry you, Azura. I simply don't love you."

"Love!" raged the queen, pacing up and down the cell. "What's love? Something in a book. We go well together, Flash!" she shouted. "You're a fool to reject me."

"I'm being honest, Queen Azura," Flash said quietly. "We would quarrel every day of the week, every hour of the day."

"No, I can be very nice to my king," Azura said.

Flash rubbed his chin thoughtfully. "What happened between you and Ming, Azura?"

She backed away, staring at him in cold fury. "He's an idiot," she said angrily. "I made a terrible mistake when I teamed up with him. Oh, he can rally the Mingolites and we can win all right, but he's going to be more trouble than he's worth on the throne."

Flash smiled.

"Don't laugh at me!" she shouted. "He might be king, and you'll be dead!"

Flash moved toward her. "You'd kill me because I wouldn't be your king?" he asked quietly.

"Yes!" she cried. "I have no further use for you. Prince Barin is in chains, ready to be killed. Once we destroy you and Barin, we will take over Arboria, and then all of Mongo."

"Your bargain with Prince Barin was simply a lie," Flash said musingly.

"Of course it was a lie!" the Queen said. "A bird in the hand—"

Flash reached up and Queen Azura felt her wrists seized by his strong hands.

"—is worth two in the bush," he said, laughing. "Take me to Prince Barin," he ordered. "We're going to set him free."

"Get away from me!" yelled Queen Azura. "How dare you—?" Her eyes widened. What had happened to the pacifist mist? How had Flash Gordon been able to rid himself of his fear? He had grabbed her boldly, and he was holding onto her so that she could not escape.

"I mean it," warned Flash. "Take me to Prince Barin and order him released, or I'll break your wrists."

Queen Azura felt fear well up in her. She could feel the hair on her head stiffen. Her throat was dry.

"You—what have you done?"

"I feel like myself for the first time since I've been in Azuria," said Flash. "I presume the drug has worn off."

Azura took a deep breath and started to scream. Flash anticipated the scream, and clapped his hand over her mouth after she had gotten out only a small cry.

"Quiet, Your Majesty," Flash said ironically, and dragged her back into the shadows of the cell with him. "If anyone comes—"

But no one did.

"Now," Flash said, pushing her forward, "we're going to go to Prince Barin."

"No," Azura retorted, "I refuse to. If I call a guard, you'll be dead in seconds."

"Not when they see that I have their queen where I can break her neck with a chop of the hand."

The strength drained out of Azura. "All right," she said, "I'll go."

"You bet you'll go," said Flash.

He started dragging her toward the cell door. "Now give me that key and no tricks."

"I promise," she said meekly.

She fumbled in a small bag she carried at her belt and finally opened it. Tears of rage flowed out of her eyes and down her cheeks.

"You're hurting me, Flash," she said, sobbing.

He did not let go of her wrists.

Then, suddenly, she had a small knife in her hand and

she spun around toward him, aiming the cutting edge at his bare chest.

Flash let go of her and drew back quickly to protect himself.

She slipped through the cell door and slammed it shut from the outside.

Angrily Flash grabbed the bars and stared out at her.

"And for that little bit of rebellion, my dear Earthling," Azura snarled, "you'll pay with your life!"

Flash gazed helplessly at her.

"Jado!" she called. "Come here immediately! I have work for you."

There was an answering voice from down the corridor. Azura turned and watched as the husky courier came down the passageway toward her.

"Jado," she said. "There has been a change of plan. The Earthman will be put to death immediately. Inform the guards on the execution team right away."

"Yes, Your Majesty," said Jado. He glanced at the window through which Flash Gordon's face was visible.

"Quickly, Jado," ordered the queen. "Be on your way!" She turned from him and started off down the corridor.

"Yes, oh, queen!" Jado said in a low voice.

Azura was puzzled by the strange quality of Jado's tone. She was about to turn and study him more closely when she felt his arm close around her neck. And than a muffler was pressed so tightly to her mouth that she could not speak.

"Help!" she tried to scream.

"Sorry about this, Your Majesty," Jado said in an amused voice.

She kicked at his legs in exasperation.

Chapter 20

Flash Gordon gripped the bars of the window in his cell door, and stared through them in astonishment at the strange antics of the guard who had fed him. It seemed to Flash that nothing made sense anymore—nothing that had happened for as long as he had been in Azuria with the glamorous Witch Queen.

Now, with the guard gripping the queen in the crook of his arm and stuffing a muffler down her throat, Flash knew that there was a deeper game afoot than he knew about.

The struggling guard turned and moved Queen Azura closer to the barred window.

"Flash!" he called out.

Flash straightened. He recognized that voice. It was Prince Barin's—quite recognizable even after the six years in which he had not heard it. But how?

"It's me," said the guard. "I'm Prince Barin. It's a cosmetic disguise. I didn't mean to tip off the masquerade just yet, but events have begun to accelerate. We've got to get out of here—fast!"

"I understand," said Flash.

"You were drugged," Prince Barin explained quickly. "I gave you an antidote."

Now Flash knew what had happened. "Right," Flash said. "We can use Queen Azura to escape, but first we've got to rescue Willie."

There was a sound of voices in the corridor.

"What's that?" Prince Barin asked in dismay.

Flash strained his ears.

He heard: "Guard! The key to Flash Gordon's cell! Hurry it up!"

"It's Ming the Second," Flash told Prince Barin in a

whisper. "Take the queen," Flash ordered, "and stand by. Ming doesn't know the drug has worn off. I've been waiting for a chance like this." Flash pulled at the cell door. "Let me out in that hall a moment."

Prince Barin unlatched the cell door, still holding the queen in a tight grip. "Where shall I take her?"

"Down the corridor into another cell," said Flash. "They're all empty. This section has been reserved for me."

"Right," said Prince Barin. Barin dragged Queen Azura with him into an empty cell beyond that of Flash Gordon.

Flash ran down the corridor and stood in front of a cabinet of guardsmen's weapons near the turn. He opened the case, removed a sword, and ran back to his cell, closing the door behind him. Once inside, he quickly covered the sword with his blanket and sank into the corner, feigning his usual indolence and fright.

Soon he heard Ming's footsteps thundering down the corridor.

"Open the door, Guard!" cried Ming.

"Yes, sir," muttered a voice.

The cell door squeaked open and Ming stepped inside, with the guard bowing behind him.

"Ha!" roared Ming, staring into the corner at Flash. "Flash Gordon, my favorite jester. Come on—up! Rise and shine! It's time to amuse your emperor."

Flash cringed, but said nothing.

Ming turned in contempt, and ran his fingers up and down a long blacksnake whip he carried with him.

"You can wait outside, Guard."

"Yes, sir," said the guard and backed out.

Ming turned and eyed Flash with amusement.

"Now, Flash Gordon, mighty legend. You have no large apartment to run through to elude me. You have no Queen Azura's skirts to hide behind. Now I can make you dance to the tune my whip plays."

"Don't hurt me," Flash whispered, cowering.

Ming roared with laughter. "At last we meet on an equal basis, Flash Gordon. Now we can test ourselves with one another."

"Yes," Flash said in a low voice. "We can test ourselves with one another."

"Don't mumble, Earthling." commanded Ming. "What did you say?"

Flash rose slowly.

Ming moved backward, laughing, and cracked the whip so the tip of it exploded at Flash's feet.

"Dance, Earthling! Your emperor likes to see strong men dance!"

Flash leaped up as the whip cracked again at his boots.

Have your laughs, Ming, he thought.

Ming backed off again, coiling the whip and raising it. "Once again, mighty Earthman," Ming said, chuckling. "Let's see another of your marvelous dance steps. Queen Azura never told me you were so light and nimble on your feet. You should have been a chorus boy, Flash Gordon, instead of a space adventurer."

The whip cracked harshly and Flash jumped again.

"Not fast enough," Ming said. "Let's do that one again, Flash Gordon. Quickly. Step, step—"

He snapped the whip. Flash jumped.

Ming cackled with glee and once again coiled the whip.

Flash stared at him. Now, he thought. This is your last dance step, Ming. We'll see how you'd like to dance to my tune.

"Dance, Earthman!" cried Ming, and flicked the whip at Flash's legs. But Flash reached down and grabbed the end of the whip just before it snapped.

"You want a dance, Ming?" Flash called out, as he pulled the end of the whip toward him.

Ming, still holding the handle, was pulled off his feet and catapulted toward Flash.

"Come closer, big man," Flash said grimly.

Ming threw down the whip, staggering to regain his balance.

"The drug's worn off!" he said fearfully. "Guard!"

There was a sound outside the cell.

Flash could hear Prince Barin's tones. "Hold it."

The guard rattled at the cell door. "Yes, sir."

"No, you don't," Prince Barin called out. "You stay out here with me. That's a private quarrel."

There were sounds of a struggle in the corridor.

Ming backed off from Flash. "Guard! I'll have your life for this disobedience!"

Flash moved toward Ming. "Your guard won't help, Ming. He's neutralized."

"But—?"

"You've been wanting to test me. Let's try it now, shall we? On an equal footing."

Ming rallied. He straightened, and drew the hidden sword he carried from its sheath under his tunic.

"Still the fool, Flash. Drug or no, I'll call the terms. My sword against your"—his eyes moved to the floor of the cell—"whip?"

He laughed loudly and lunged toward Flash.

Flash moved quickly, ripping the blanket from the sword he had taken from the guard's cabinet in the corridor.

"Ah-ha!" Ming said. "So the tricky Flash Gordon has once again resumed his famed ingeniousness, has he?"

"I'm ready, Ming. How about you?"

"I've been waiting for this moment," Ming chortled.

"Then let's have it!" cried Flash.

"If you're ready to face your death—!" Ming swung his sword at Flash.

"Well, Ming Jr.," said Flash, "you've wanted a showdown. Now you have it."

Ming chuckled. "You'll be sniveling like a puppy again before I'm done with you, Flash Gordon."

Ming slashed and Flash pulled back, returning the thrust.

"Save your breath for the fight, Ming!" he said, laughing.

Ming darted to the side, thrusting again.

Flash parried the thrust and flipped Ming's sword to the floor.

Ming backed away in terror. "My sword!"

Flash advanced and picked up Ming's sword. "A lifetime of training for this encounter and you're no better than that, little Ming?"

Ming's face swelled with rage. "You don't call me little Ming, you Earth monster!" screamed Ming.

Flash threw Ming's sword in the corner.

"You wouldn't attack an unarmed man," said Flash, and threw his own sword over his shoulder.

"But, but—"

"This is a job I'd like to do by hand!" Flash thundered, and crouched in a boxer's stance.

Ming smiled faintly. "I'm your match any day, Earthman," said Ming, crouching like Flash.

Flash moved in, keeping his feet moving.

Ming backed off, watching for an opening.

Flash feinted with his left. Ming started to react, but

saw Flash's expression and back-pedaled with an arrogant smile.

"None of your tricks, pugilist," sneered Ming.

Flash laughed. "I haven't seen your style yet, Ming."

Ming feinted with his left, then drove in with his right. Flash parried. Ming came in with a haymaker, using his left, and Flash let him land one blow to his shoulder.

Happily, Ming leaped back.

Flash grinned. He bobbed forward and drew one parry by Ming, stepped to the right, feinted. Then to the left and landed a quick right jab, then a left jab, which was blocked, and a hard right to the jaw, which staggered Ming slightly.

Then Flash came in with a quick left-and-right combination, and a left. Ming moved backward against the wall, pumping his legs furiously.

As Flash lunged in for the kill, Ming suddenly crouched, spun, and attacked Flash's uncovered chest with three triphammer blows that staggered him and threw him off-balance.

Overconfident, Flash thought.

He went down, but immediately on touching the floor uncoiled and sprang to his feet.

Ming, thinking that Flash had been battered to the floor, came in on top of him, reaching out to land the *coup de grace*.

Flash leaped to his feet, coming in on Ming's exposed neck with a karate chop.

Ming went down hard.

Flash called out, "Barin, are you out there?"

"Yes," Prince Barin called.

"Have the queen release Willie from the suspension vault."

"Right," said Prince Barin through the cell door.

"I'll truss up Ming and be right with you."

"Excellent," said Prince Barin.

Flash heard steps retreating down the corridor.

Ming was shaking his head, clawing at the stone of the cell floor, trying to clear his vision.

"Come on, Ming," said Flash, moving over to him. "Get on your feet! I'm going to put you where you'll be safe for a while."

"Flash," whimpered Ming, "I've had enough. No more. Please!"

Flash laughed, pulling Ming to his feet. "Hands on top of your head, Ming," he ordered.

Slowly, Ming placed his hands on top of the helmet he wore.

"So?" Flash asked. "You mean you've run out of your slippery tricks? All right, Ming. I don't have the same stomach as you do for brutality. Just come quietly with me."

"You are a man of honor, Flash Gordon," Ming said abjectly.

Flash smiled. "Let's go."

Quickly Ming twisted his hands, removed the helmet from his head, and slammed it at Flash.

"And I salute you!" shouted Ming, diving for the floor and one of the swords lying there.

Flash was driven back by the fury of the blow, and crashed against the wall. The helmet struck him in the cheek, drawing blood and clouding his vision. It then clattered to the floor.

Flash slumped against the wall and slid to the stones, momentarily stunned.

Ming leaped, his sword aimed directly at Flash's heart.

Chapter 21

Grasping the guard tightly and holding his thumb on a pressure point in the guard's neck, Prince Barin propelled the Azurian down the corridor and pushed him into the cell where he had left Queen Azura.

"All right, soldier," Barin said menacingly. "In you go. And stay quiet, if you value your life!"

"Yes, sir," said the guard, frowning. "But why does a loyal courier of the queen's turn against not only the queen, but her loyal ally, too?"

Barin laughed. He turned to Queen Azura, who was sitting, quite subdued, on the prisoner's cot in the corner.

"It is a fair question, is it not, Queen Azura?"

"What Jado?" the queen asked faintly.

Barin walked over and stood above the queen. He was frowning slightly. "You seem to have been bitten by the same drug you gave Flash Gordon, Queen Azura."

Azura lifted her head and stared at Barin and he could see the fear in her eyes.

"What did you say, Jado?"

Barin frowned and then laughed. "With whom did you dine last, Queen Azura?"

"I dined with Ming, of course," she replied without hesitation. "Qilp served us and—"

"Qilp!" Barin suddenly saw the whole plot. "But of course! And you richly deserve what happened, Queen Azura. Don't you see what they've done to you?"

"I have no idea what you're talking about," the Queen replied, but her heart was not in it.

"But it's true! You are under the effect of the drug you were using on Flash Gordon! Somehow Ming got Qilp to serve you the drug, so he could take over the Kingdom of the Blue Magic, kill Flash Gordon and Prince Barin, and become emperor of your people! Then he would move your troops into Arboria, take over the Free Council of Mongo, and rule the planet!"

The queen's expression was a combination of sudden understanding—rage, fear, and absolute terror.

"He—he wouldn't—and Qilp—Qilp wouldn't."

"I'm afraid he did, Queen Azura. You know it, but you can't fight back because of the drug."

Tears ran down her cheeks. "Jado, I trust you."

Prince Barin began removing the makeup his cosmeticians had applied in Arboria. Slowly, before her eyes, he changed from the faithful Jado into her old adversary, Prince Barin.

Queen Azura's eyes widened and her face again broke up into a mask of aversion and terror.

"No! I can't believe it! You're Prince Barin!"

Barin smiled. "In person, Queen Azura. And we're going up to release the Earth teenager from the suspension vault."

Azura cowered.

Barin grasped her by the arm and lifted her from the cot. She rose, trembling, her hand held fearfully to her mouth.

"Guard, if I hear so much as a peep out of you, I'll have you killed," said Prince Barin, and, pulling Queen Azura after him, slammed the door of the cell shut, the noise echoing along the entire corridor.

In the darkened hallway, he held Queen Azura closely to him and looked her in the eye.

"Now, Queen Azura, lead me to the suspension vault, if you please."

Queen Azura, unable to act against Prince Barin, and shaking in terror, accompanied him through the winding corridors of the palace to her suite.

Guards stiffened to attention as she passed, and Barin made sure that she did not attempt to signal any of them. She was totally subdued, a tribute to the drug which she had encouraged her scientists to perfect for her.

"It should interest you, Queen Azura," he whispered at one point, "how effective your anti-courage drug is, particularly when applied to the one who used it with such success on Flash Gordon."

The queen was not amused, but she was unable to turn her apprehension and fear into anger and action against

Prince Barin. She continued to cower beside him as she led him into the chamber of the suspension vaults.

Willie stood in the vault—the boy whom Prince Barin had just heard about from Flash Gordon.

"Guard!" shouted Prince Barin. "The queen wishes the boy released from the nerve drug."

One of several guards approached and saluted the queen. "Yes, Your Majesty?"

Prince Barin prodded her. "Yes," Queen Azura said dreamily. "Do as he says."

"Release the boy from the drug," snapped Prince Barin.

The guard nodded, went across the room to a cupboard, removed a jar from the shelf, and brought the potion over to the suspension vault.

Within seconds, Willie's eyes flickered and he smiled at Prince Barin.

"Who are you?" he asked.

Prince Barin stood quietly watching him. "I'm Prince Barin, lad. Are you Gordon's young companion?"

"Yes, sir," said the boy. "Gee. You're Prince Barin? I've heard about you."

"And I about you," said Prince Barin.

"Where's Flash Gordon?"

"In another part of the palace," said the Prince.

"Hey! I wish we were there with him," Willie said.

Prince Barin blinked in astonishment.

No sooner said than done. They were in Flash Gordon's cell and—

The moment he had fallen to the floor, Flash understood exactly how Ming had tricked him with the helmet. But he was powerless to bring his adversary to judgment.

Ming lunged at him, the sword flashing.

Flash rolled quickly out of the way.

Ming laughed, once again recovering his stance. "You should have killed me when you had the chance, you merciful fool!" he gloated, waving the sword.

Flash stretched out his hand for the second sword which lay over a foot away from his outstretched hand.

Ming's foot stamped on Flash's wrist.

"No!" he said. "I'm not going to let you have another chance at me!" He raised the sword in his hand and brought it down toward Flash's shoulder.

"Oh, no," Flash said, countering by flipping over and stabbing up with his booted foot at Ming's knee.

Ming went backward, the sword flying loose.

"I've got a few tricks left, Ming, before I cash in!" Flash cried.

Ming went down on his back, hard. As he hit the floor, he reached for the sword he had lost.

"No, you don't!" exclaimed Flash. "We're going to have this out hand to hand."

Flash jumped on Ming and foiled his attempt to reach for the sword.

"Hands?" Ming growled, as Flash rose, holding Ming's forearm to bring him to his feet. "How about feet? That gentle art of 'savate' as you call it on Earth?"

Ming smashed his foot into Flash's solar plexus.

Flash fell, crumpled to the floor in pain.

"You can't run now, Flash," Ming crowed in triumph. "You're finished."

He reached for the sword, got it, and straightened up to deliver the final blow to Flash Gordon.

Willie stared in dismay at the scene before his eyes. He saw Flash Gordon on the floor of a dismal prison cell, with a big bearded man standing over him.

I wish you'd stop, Willie thought.

Instantly the big man stood stone-still, frozen in time and space.

Flash Gordon glanced up at Willie, saw him, and smiled faintly.

"Willie," he said sighing. "You've saved my life again!"

Queen Azura stared in disbelief. "Magic," she muttered. "Real magic!"

Flash rose, removed the sword from Ming the Second's hand, and threw it to the floor.

"Ming," he said sadly, "it looks like you're going to have to be put away for the safety of the planet."

"Amen to that," said Prince Barin, walking toward Flash with Queen Azura in tow.

"Willie," said Flash, "get me some rope."

"Okay, Mr. Gordon," Willie said obediently and ran out.

Flash stared at Queen Azura; then he frowned at Prince Barin.

"Barin, what's the matter with the queen? She seems totally subdued."

"So much so that I had no trouble at all finding Willie

and bringing him out of the effects of the nerve gas, which is called paralysis mist, according to Queen Azura."

"How do you account for the queen's docility?" Flash asked, again staring at the beautiful Azura.

Prince Barin laughed. "The truth of the matter seems to be that Ming the Second found out about the drug that had been used on you, and procured some of it for himself. When Azura began leaning on him because of his treatment of you, he resented it.

"The nearest thing I can figure out is that he decided to turn the drug against the queen, and give a delayed-action dose of it to her. He figured to kill Prince Barin"—Barin smiled and waved his hand—"that false one in the torture chamber, and then kill you. After that, he would be in control of Azuria and Arboria and the Free Council. He would be ruler of Mongo."

"Who helped him?" Flash asked.

"The dwarf, Qilp," Prince Barin said, laughing. "His cousin!"

"How'd you know about him,?" Flash was puzzled.

"You forget that I've got it all stored in my memory under Jado's memory bank."

Flash grinned. "Son of a gun," he said. "That's right. You do know all about the palace intrigues."

"I also know that Jado himself wanted to overthrow the queen. Only he figured he would do it for himself, and not cut in Ming."

"It gets so you can't trust anybody." Flash sighed. He turned to Azura. "You heard all that?"

"Yes, Flash," she said in a low voice. "What are you going to do with me?"

"I haven't figured it out, yet," Flash said thoughtfully.

Willie ran in with a length of rope and started to tie up Ming the Second.

It was a sunny afternoon on the dining balcony of the palace in Arboria. At table were Flash Gordon, Dr. Zarkov, Prince Barin, Dale Arden, and Willie.

"Hey, ice cream!" Worriless Willie cried in ecstasy.

"Just for you," Barin said. "Doc Zarkov told me about your sweet tooth."

"Gee! It's the best dessert there is!" He plunged in and the rest of them laughed.

"Well," said Zarkov, turning to Prince Barin, "how goes the Kingdom of Arboria?"

Barin relaxed, smiling. "The Free Council is convinced that we have no more worries about the secret army Queen Azura was mounting against us."

"And the queen?"

"The effects of the delayed-action drug administered by Ming the Second and Qilp have worn off. She's as mean as ever—it's just her nature—but I think she'll behave herself for some time to come. We threw a pretty big scare into her, you know."

Zarkov shook his head. "What frightens me is the existence of Ming the Second! Can you imagine that? Nobody knew Ming the Merciless had a son."

"Oh, there were rumors for years," Barin said slowly. "We just didn't follow them up as we should have."

"He ought to have been executed," Zarkov snorted.

"No," said Prince Barin. "The Free Council has acted on him already. He's to be kept in prison under the aegis of the council itself. Even if he were killed, we would have others coming up pretending to be descendants of Ming. No, it's best to have the real Ming the Second where we can watch him."

"Maybe," said Zarkov.

"I never did understand about that personality transference," Dale said. "What happened to the real Azurian courier?"

"Jado?" Prince Barin smiled. "Well, we rescued him from the torture chamber and brought him back here to Arboria to undergo transference in reverse. He's back to normal, and working for the queen now."

"I would have executed him," Zarkov said darkly.

"You're a blood-thirsty tyrant, Doc," Prince Barin said good-naturedly. "I know Jado has plans to become ruler of Azuria, as king to the queen, but it's only a dream. Nobody thinks it can happen."

Zarkov shook his head. "Weak-kneed administration of justice," he snorted.

"Whatever happened to that capering dwarf, Qilp?" Flash Gordon asked after a moment's silence.

"Well, he's still the queen's right-hand man, but the rumor is that she's keeping him under heavy security so he can't turn against her ever again."

"I would have given him the fear drug—pacifist mist as they call it—and let him be her vassal," said Zarkov.

Prince Barin looked stern. "You're being silly, Doc. We took all the formulations and pills we found in the Blue

Magic laboratories and put them to the torch out in the middle of the Great Mongo Desert. Scientifically speaking, Queen Azura's right back where she started."

"I wouldn't trust her too far," Flash warned. "She did it once, and she can do it again."

"But not for a while," Prince Barin said.

Dale turned to Willie. "How's that ice cream?"

"Swell," Willie said, grinning at her.

"Willie, when are we going home?" Dale asked in a soft voice. "I've got work to do."

Willie's face fell. "Gee, I didn't think we would want to go back for a while, Miss Arden."

Dale raised an eyebrow. "Oh, come on, Willie! You've had enough adventures for a lifetime, haven't you?"

Willie's face assumed a vacant expression, and they could all tell that he was daydreaming again.

"Hey," he said. "It's really exciting here on Mongo. You know?"

"What's exciting, Willie?" Prince Barin asked tensely.

"Trouble," said Willie, his face lighting up. "Big trouble. Far away from Arboria. I kind of wish we—"